LAW OF THE PRAIRIE

Wayne C. Lee was born to pioneering homesteaders near Lamar, Nebraska. His parents were old when he was born and it was an unwritten law since the days of the frontier that it was expected that the youngest child would care for the parents in old age. Having grown up reading novels by Zane Grey and William MacLeod Raine, Lee wanted to write Western stories himself. His best teachers were his parents. They might not be able to remember what happened last week by the time Lee had reached his majority, but they shared with him their very clear memories of the pioneer days. In fact they talked so much about that period that it sometimes seemed to Lee he had lived through it himself. Lee wrote a short story and let his mother read it. She encouraged him to submit it to a magazine and said she would pay the postage. It was accepted and appeared as *Death Waits at Paradise Pass* in *Lariat Story Magazine*. In the many Western novels that he has written since, violence has never been his primary focus, no matter what title a publisher might give one of his stories, but rather the interrelationships between the characters and within their communities. These are the dominant characteristics in all of Lee's Western fiction and create the ambiance so memorable in such diverse narratives as *The Gun Tamer* (1963), *Petticoat Wagon Train* (1972), and *Arikaree War Cry* (1992). In the truest sense Wayne C. Lee's Western fiction is an outgrowth of his impulse to create imaginary social fabrics on the frontier and his stories are intended primarily to entertain a reader at the same time as to articulate what it was about these pioneering men and women that makes them so unique and intriguing to later generations. His pacing, graceful style, natural sense of humor, and the genuine liking he feels toward the majority of his characters, combined with a commitment to the reality and power of romance between men and women as a decisive factor in making it possible for them to have a better life together than they could ever hope to have apart, are what most distinguish his contributions to the Western story. His latest novel is *Edge of Nowhere* (1996).

LAW OF THE PRAIRIE

Wayne C. Lee

GUNSMOKE

First published in the US by Lennox Hill

This hardback edition 2011
by AudioGO Ltd
by arrangement with
Golden West Literary Agency

ISBN 978 1 445 85632 2

British Library Cataloguing in Publication Data available.

Printed and bound in Great Britain by
CPI Antony Rowe, Chippenham and Eastbourne

LAW OF THE PRAIRIE

1.

It was a dismal way to start September. Troy Prescott's father, Frank, had been killed just yesterday, and now, at the funeral, was no time for Troy to think about all the changes this was going to mean for him.

Troy had often heard remarks about blue Monday, but Tuesday, August 30, 1898, would be the day he would always remember as the saddest day of his life.

As the procession made its way slowly from the church in Peaceful Springs to the cemetery a long mile west of town, Troy, riding in the spring wagon immediately behind the hearse, knew that his mourning would have to end when the ceremonies were over at the graveside. In addition to his own problems and those his father had left, he intended to make sure his father's killer came to justice.

Troy tried to remember who had been in the crowd at the church. The little church at Peaceful Springs wasn't big, and Frank Prescott had been so well known and liked that much of the crowd hadn't been able to get inside. Besides, a sudden unexpected death, especially a murder, always brought out the curious as well as the true mourners.

Troy doubted if a list of everyone at the funeral would be of any real help to him. He knew Frank's real friends. And most of the others present were there out of curiosity. The one who had killed Frank Prescott wasn't likely to be at the funeral.

Troy had his own idea who that was. But none of the Detts had been at the funeral; Troy would bet on that. Rafe Dett had done everything but threaten to kill Frank Prescott if he didn't sell his land to him. Frank had refused to sell, and he had died.

The procession reached the cemetery and turned in at the north gate. It wasn't an old cemetery; the community wasn't old. But there were already several graves there. The hearse stopped near an open grave which had been dug beside another grave with only a few weeds on it to show that it was no more than a year or two old. Hard work and pneumonia had claimed Troy's mother the winter before last. Now her husband would lie beside her, and only murder could be listed as the cause of his death.

8

The ceremonies were brief as the people crowded around the open grave with the casket sitting on the stretched ropes that would later lower it into the grave. Troy only half listened to the minister give a final eulogy and hold out the promise of meeting the departed in the next world.

Then the people began to turn away to their teams and buggies and spring wagons. But some stayed to visit for a while.

Two dozen close friends and neighbors came past Troy to shake his hand and mumble some words that were intended to comfort him. He returned the handclasps but didn't listen to the words. They had little meaning for him now. Nothing mattered except to right the terrible wrong that had been committed.

Morrie Grote, who had worked for Frank Prescott on the ranch southeast of Peaceful Springs, came by and gripped Troy's hand. Troy understood. He and Morrie were just the same age, twenty-four, and Morrie had taken up the extra work on the ranch when Troy left to open his real estate office in Peaceful Springs. They had been friends before Troy left the ranch. Now they would be closer than ever.

"Don't you think it is time to get away from here?" Morrie asked. "Most everybody has had a chance to come by and tell you how sorry they are."

Troy nodded. "I've been wishing for a reason to get

9

away. We've got things to do, you know."

"Sure, I know," Morrie said. "But you don't want to go off half cocked on this. We've got enough trouble as it is."

"You know as well as I do that Rafe Dett shot Pa," Troy said, feeling his anger rise at the sound of Rafe's name.

"Knowing and proving are two different things, as the sheriff says." Morrie started toward the spring wagon Troy had come in, then stopped. "Here come Mary and Doris. They'll be hurt if you don't wait to speak to them."

Mary Willouby was the recorder of deeds at the courthouse in Peaceful Springs, and Doris Jewel was the teacher at the school nearby. She had taught there last year and boarded with Mary and had come back a few days early this fall to get ready for another school term. They were two of the best friends the Prescott family had.

"If there is anything we can do to help, Troy, just call on us," Mary said. "We know you'll have a lot of things to straighten out at the ranch."

"I reckon I will," Troy said. "I won't forget that you are a professional at straightening out things."

Doris said nothing, but Troy knew that didn't mean she wasn't as willing and eager to help as Mary. To her, unnecessary words were as useless as wasted minutes spent watching the clock approach recess time.

Sheriff Robert Hanson came striding past the spring wagon as Troy got in. "We'll find out who did it, Troy," he promised.

"You know who did it," Troy said hotly. "Rafe Dett. He's the only one who had any reason to kill Pa."

"Now don't go flying off the handle," the sheriff warned. "Nobody saw Rafe do it."

"You don't have to see a skunk to tell he's in the chicken coop," Troy snapped. "If you don't do something about him, I will."

"Hold on!" Hanson said sharply. "I'll go so far as to say that I personally agree with you that Rafe is the prime suspect. But as sheriff, I have to have proof. And right now, I don't have a shred of proof that Rafe killed Frank."

"He's not going to get away with it, Sheriff," Troy said. "He's the kind who thinks he can bull his way over anybody who tries to stop him. And he wants that land Pa owned between his two pieces."

"I know all that," Hanson said. "And I'm going to ask Rafe a lot of questions. But in the meantime, you keep your nose clean. Understand?"

Troy nodded as the sheriff walked on. Morrie picked up the reins.

"You can't afford to get Hanson on the prod, Troy," he said.

"Can't let Rafe get off scot-free, either," Troy said. He looked at Mary and Doris, still standing close to the spring wagon. "Want a lift back to town?"

"We've got our own buggy," Mary said quickly. "But you listen to Morrie. The sheriff will question Rafe."

"And Rafe will have a perfect alibi," Troy said. "The sheriff may be just a bit easy, too. There'll soon be an election. And the county seat could be moved to Mapleton. You know who runs things over there— Jake Dett."

A worried frown crossed Mary Willouby's brow. "I know. But before there can be a special county seat election, they have to get two thirds of the property owners in the county to sign that petition. They didn't get that many the last time they tried."

"From what I hear, they're giving it a harder try this time," Troy said.

"We'll beat them in the election if they succeed with the petition," Doris said as if that ended the matter.

Morrie swung the team around to the north gate of the cemetery, then turned east toward town. Troy sat in silence, trying to sort out his thoughts. The sheriff was right, of course. He didn't dare lift a finger against Rafe Dett, although he was positive that Rafe was the one who had killed Frank Prescott. It was going to be hard to sit by and watch Rafe run loose and not do a thing about it. But he'd have no choice.

One thing was certain: Rafe would not get the Prescott ranch now. Troy was an only child. His mother and father were both dead, so that ranch would be his. And he'd fight to his dying breath before he'd let a Dett lay claim to it.

There were other things he'd inherit now, too. His father had bought a lot of property in Peaceful Springs when he saw the town gradually fading away. Troy didn't know whether it was his faith in the future of the town or just stubborn pride that made him buy the property to keep Peaceful Springs going. Troy had to cling to that same determination.

He had set up his real estate office in town because Frank had convinced him that Peaceful Springs had a great future. As long as the county seat stayed there, Troy couldn't see how the town could fade away much more. There were fewer than a hundred residents now. Mapleton, over in the extreme corner of the county, had been trying to get the county seat away from Peaceful Springs ever since it had been located there. Mapleton was a much bigger town. But Peaceful Springs was in the center of the county, and it had a fine courthouse. It had been a running battle between those factors and the density of population in

Mapleton every time the subject of the county seat came up.

As the spring wagon came into town, it passed the huge stone and brick courthouse and the schoolhouse. Both had been gifts of a benefactor back when the county was organized. The gifts were to be made only if Peaceful Springs was made the permanent county seat. When the town won the county seat election with more votes than all its rivals combined, the courthouse and schoolhouse were finished and put into use.

"Let's stop at the hotel," Troy said.

Morrie nodded and headed down the street east of the courthouse that crossed West Spring Creek and came up to the hotel, which stood close to the north end of the business section of town. The church where the funeral had been held was just to the north of the hotel.

The hotel was one of the properties Frank Prescott had bought when it had gone up for sale. The grocery store was another. Frank had Al and Emma Theim running the hotel for him and Ken Carlander operating the store. The responsibilities for both of these would fall on Troy now.

Al Theim, a tall lean man with thinning brown hair and watery blue eyes, came out on the veranda of the hotel when Troy and Morrie drove up.

"I'm sorry I had to miss the funeral," he said. "But

14

somebody had to keep an eye on things here."

"Where's Betsy?" Troy asked.

Betsy Theim was just a year younger than Troy, and he and Betsy had been keeping company for nearly a year now. Betsy was a slim golden-haired girl with bright blue eyes inherited from her mother.

"Em and Betsy went to the funeral," Al Theim said. "I heard them drive in the back just a while ago. Reckon you'll have to wait a minute if you want to see Betsy."

Troy sighed. "I'm not sure just what I do want. I've got a lot on my mind."

"Reckon you would have," Al said. "We've been a mite worried, too, about this talk of another county seat election. If we lose the county seat to Mapleton, this hotel won't get half a dozen customers a year. We make most of our money when court is in session. No place else for anybody to stay."

Emma Theim came to the front door alone. Al frowned as he looked at his wife.

"Where's Betsy?" he demanded.

"She saddled her horse and went for a ride," Emma said, and Troy detected uneasiness in her voice. "Said the funeral depressed her, and she wanted to wear it off."

"She could have done more good staying here and talking to Troy," Al said.

"I don't blame her," Troy said. "I feel like getting

off by myself and trying to figure things out, too. Let's go, Morrie."

"Seems like Betsy's been doing a lot of riding around the country lately," Morrie muttered as he swung the team south down Grand Avenue. They passed the grocery store, but it was still closed. Ken Carlander and his wife had been at the funeral. Most of the town's businesses had closed for the funeral, and some of them were just opening their doors now.

At the little office where he handled his real estate business, Troy called a halt and unlocked the front door. Inside, he went to his desk and pulled out a drawer. Two revolvers, a .45 and a .32, were there, the .32 a gift from his father when Troy was twelve years old. He hadn't used either revolver even for target practice for a long time. But now he jammed the .45 under his waistband.

He looked around his office, thinking that his business there could soon vanish if Mapleton were successful in wresting the county seat from Peaceful Springs. Business had been pretty slack lately, anyway. Troy could remember when there had been such high hopes for the town that lots had been selling for fancy prices. But his father had bought the hotel and grocery store recently for less than the buildings were worth. The land they were sitting on was just thrown in. Most of Troy's real estate transactions were in ranch and farm land near town.

The weight of the gun sagging in his belt was too heavy, and Troy yanked out another drawer and got the belt that went with the gun. Strapping it on, he shifted the uncomfortable weight around until it didn't seem quite so awkward, then went back out to where Morrie was waiting.

"Going to stay at the ranch now?" Morrie asked.

Troy nodded. He had stayed at the ranch part of the time, anyway, since it was only a little over a mile southeast of town along the Smoky Hill River. He had kept a room at the hotel, too, but now that the operation of the ranch was his responsibility, he'd stay out there all the time.

They turned east on Spruce Street and crossed East Spring Creek, which was dry now, then headed southeast toward the ranch. There Morrie put up the team, while Troy lifted the gun from its holster, tested the grip, then fired the gun a few times at the corner post of the corral. If Rafe Dett would kill his father to get the place, as Troy firmly believed, why wouldn't he try to kill Troy, too? Over in Mapleton, Jake Dett was a big wheel. Since his wife had inherited money from her father, who had owned some big business in Kansas City, Jake had been riding high, buying land as if he expected to own all of St. George County one of these days.

Apparently he felt that the Detts could get away with whatever was necessary for their expansion. After buying the two small ranches on either side of the Prescott ranch, they had been trying to buy Frank Prescott's land. As Troy saw it, when they had failed to get Frank to sell, they had killed him. It was as simple as that. But killing Frank Prescott wasn't going to get the ranch for the Detts. Not as long as Troy lived. And Troy wondered if the Detts wouldn't figure things the same way.

He shoved the gun back in its holster and went into the house and crossed the room to the little safe his father used. Troy had never been allowed to use the safe; that was his father's one bit of untouchable privacy. It took Troy ten minutes to find the combination to the safe hidden in a pigeonhole in his father's writing desk.

Using the numbers, he had to try several times before he discovered which way to turn the dial between numbers. But the safe door finally yielded to his touch.

There wasn't much in the safe; only about a hundred dollars in money and a neat pile of papers. Troy ignored the money and began on the papers. Before he had gone halfway through them, he realized that things had not been going as well with his father as he had supposed.

The rent he received from the hotel and store had barely paid the taxes. The upkeep on the buildings had been coming out of his pocket. But more shocking was the mortgage on the ranch that he discovered. The mortgage was held by the bank in Dodge City. Apparently Frank hadn't wanted any local people to know he was in financial trouble. Frank had been a proud man, determined to keep alive his dream that Peaceful Springs would be a great city one day. He had mortgaged his ranch to buy property in town to keep businesses open that otherwise might close.

Squatting on his heels in front of the safe, Troy gave some quick thought to his position. His real estate business was doing fairly well. But he was going to have to make it pay off much better, and he'd have to make the ranch yield good returns or he'd never be able to meet the payments on the mortgage. If he lost the ranch, the Detts would find it easy enough to buy the land. Troy would work his fingers off to keep that from happening.

He was still crouched before the safe when the door behind him opened. Thinking it was Morrie, he didn't even turn around. But the voice that he heard made him wheel around, losing his balance and almost toppling to the floor. He was on his feet in an instant, facing the sheriff.

"I hate to do this, Troy," Sheriff Robert Hanson said. "But I've got to put you under arrest."

"Arrest?" Troy yelled. "What for?"

"For murdering Rafe Dett."

2.

For a long moment, Troy simply stared at the sheriff. If the lawman was joking, it didn't show in his face.

"You'll have to spell that out, sheriff," he said at last. "If Rafe Dett is dead, I can't say I'm sorry. But there's no way I could have killed him."

"You were telling me less than two hours ago that you'd do something to Rafe if I didn't."

It hit Troy then that the sheriff was absolutely serious. Rafe Dett must be dead, and Troy was being accused of murdering him.

"I haven't had time even to look for Rafe, much less kill him," Troy said slowly.

"You've had time enough," the sheriff said. "He was killed less than a mile from here, right on the line between your land and his. Give me your gun—carefully."

Frowning, Troy eased the gun out of his holster and handed it, butt first, to the sheriff. He wished now that he had left it in the drawer in his office in town.

"If you didn't kill Rafe or hadn't figured on it, how come you were wearing your gun?" Hanson asked. "I can't remember seeing you wear it before."

"I figured if Rafe would kill my pa just to get this land, he'd do the same to me for the same reason. With both of us dead, there wouldn't be much standing in the way of his getting this ranch."

The sheriff turned the gun around and sniffed the barrel. "It's been fired in the last hour or so. How do you explain that?"

"I shot at the corner post of the corral a couple of times just to get the feel of it again," Troy said.

"Or at Rafe Dett," Hanson said. "Come along, Troy, I'm going to have to lock you up."

Troy wondered where Morrie was. Not that it made a great deal of difference. Troy wouldn't try to escape from the sheriff even with Morrie's help. That would be a sure sign of guilt. But there must be some way to make the sheriff see he was innocent. Morrie could help do that.

"Put your stuff back in the safe and lock it," Hanson said. "I don't like doing this, Troy. But even you can see how it looks to the law."

Troy shook his head. "All I can see is that you're

making a fool of yourself. Morrie was with me every minute from the time I left the funeral till I came in the house."

"Where is he now?"

Troy shrugged. "He took the team to the barn. I haven't seen him since. Just how long has Rafe been dead?"

"Not more than half an hour, I'd say," Hanson said.

"You sure found him fast."

Hanson nodded. "I was riding out to talk to him like I told you I would. I found him when I saw his horse standing there without a rider."

"Shot with a rifle?"

The sheriff shook his head. "Shot with a pistol. At close range, too. There were powder burns on his shirt."

Troy frowned. "Who could have gotten that close to him?"

"Somebody surprised or tricked him," Hanson said. "His gun wasn't even fired. It's a plain case of murder." The sheriff stepped back to the door. "Come on, Troy. Unless you can prove where you were during the last hour, I'll have to put you in jail."

Troy realized how it must look to the sheriff. Robert Hanson had always been a good friend of the Prescotts, but this went beyond friendship.

He put the papers he had been examining back in the safe, along with his father's money, and locked the door, stuffing the combination into his pocket. Then he stepped outside as the sheriff kept his gun on him.

Morrie was coming out of the barn, and Troy called for him to bring his horse. Morrie stared for a moment in disbelief, then hurried back into the barn without a word. A couple of minutes later, he appeared leading Troy's saddled horse.

Troy let the sheriff tell Morrie what had happened. Morrie only shook his head in disagreement.

"You'll have to look after things till I get back," Troy said.

"Reckon I'll do a little more than that," Morrie said. "I know you ain't been out of the house since we got home, so there's no sense in you sitting in jail while the fellow who killed Rafe is running loose."

"You watch what you do," the sheriff warned, then motioned for Troy to head for town.

Troy rode ahead of the sheriff in silence till they were almost to town. Then he turned to face the officer.

"I suppose you'll send word to Jake Dett?"

"I'll have to. Can't keep a thing like this from him."

"He'll be over here in short order," Troy said. "You know him. He'll raise thunder and prop it up with a stick."

"Reckon he will, all right," Hanson said. "But he's got to come over and take care of his own son's body."

Troy said no more. The sheriff directed Troy through the southern end of town rather than down Broadway. When they were directly south of the courthouse square, they turned north.

The jail was a frame building to the south of the stone and brick courthouse. The sheriff and Troy dismounted, and the sheriff produced some keys and unlocked the jail. There were no other prisoners now, so Troy had the jail to himself. He was put in a cell with a small barred window high in the south wall.

"When do you figure Jake Dett will get here?" Troy asked.

The sheriff studied him for a moment. "I know you're thinking that he'll get a mob and hang you. Well, let me tell you he won't. I haven't even sent word to him yet. I'll get Herman to ride over to Mapleton and tell him. It's about twenty-four or five miles if he cuts straight across. So Jake won't be here till tomorrow."

"What about Rafe? If he's dead like you say, are you going to leave him out there?"

"Of course not," the sheriff said disgustedly. "I'll have Lew bring him in and do what has to be done till Jake gets here. I figure Jake will insist on the undertaker from Mapleton taking care of him."

The sheriff went outside, and Troy dropped down on the hard cot in the cell. Two hours before he'd been swearing vengeance on Rafe Dett for killing his father. Now Rafe was dead, and Troy was probing for some means of proving he hadn't killed him.

It would soon be supper time, but Troy didn't care whether they brought him anything to eat or not. However, when the sheriff brought a plate of food from the dining room at the hotel, he brought along Betsy Theim, which brightened Troy's world considerably.

"The sheriff told me what happened," Betsy said, coming to the bars of his cell while the sheriff waited at the door of the cell. "I know you didn't do it."

"Is there anything I can do?"

"You might have your pa look around for some clue as to who did do it," Troy suggested. "Finding the man who killed Rafe is about the only way I'm going to get out of this."

Betsy shook her head worriedly. "I don't think Pa would be any help. He's pretty worried about the hotel. If Peaceful Springs loses the county seat, Pa won't have a job."

"If I don't get out of here, I'll lose the hotel and he won't have a job, anyway," Troy said.

"I'll tell him," Betsy said, but there was still doubt in her voice.

She reached through the bars, and he took her

25

hand. She squeezed his fingers, and he felt the bond between them tighten. It hadn't been so strong when she first came in.

The sheriff suddenly came away from the door. "Get back, Betsy. Are you giving him something?"

She flipped her blonde hair as she wheeled to face Hanson, pulling her hand from Troy's grip. "Only a little love. That's more than anybody else will do."

Hanson frowned. "I gave you permission to talk to the prisoner, not hold hands with him."

"I'll be back tomorrow," Betsy said, giving Troy a smile as she brushed past the sheriff and went out the door.

Troy finished his supper and gave the plate back to the sheriff. He was contemplating the long night on that hard cot when more visitors came.

"Stay back from the bars," the sheriff warned as he let the visitors in. "It's getting dark enough so I can't see what you might slip to him."

"You can search us for guns and knives," Mary Willouby said sarcastically.

"Aw, I believe you when you say you ain't got any guns. But you know I've got to be careful."

"I didn't expect you to get over tonight," Troy said as Mary Willouby and Doris Jewel approached his cell.

"We didn't hear what had happened until Lew

brought in Rafe Dett's body," Mary said. "Then we heard that you'd been arrested for killing him. What do you know about it?"

"Not a thing," Troy said. "I went to the hotel, then to my office, then home, and started through Pa's papers. That's when the sheriff came and told me I'd killed Rafe Dett."

"We'll see the judge first thing in the morning and find out if we can get you out on bail," Mary said.

"I'd appreciate that," Troy said. "This cot won't be the most comfortable bed in the world. And I can't do much about getting at the truth of things while I'm locked up here."

"They can't convict you without any real evidence," Mary said.

"Tell that to Jake Dett when he comes."

"We'd better get you out of there before he shows up," Doris said.

After Mary and Doris left, the jail became quiet. Troy stretched out on the cot, but he couldn't sleep. He let his mind run through the happenings of the last few weeks. There must be some connection between this new county seat fight and the deaths of Frank Prescott and Rafe Dett. Jake Dett carried a lot of weight over in Mapleton, and he certainly had his spoon in the pot, stirring up this new campaign to move the county seat.

Peaceful Springs had been as quiet as its name for most of the summer. Then the first part of July, a group of men from Mapleton had come over to the courthouse and made a list of the names of the property owners of the county. That had alerted the residents of the community that the people of Mapleton were building the fire again, hoping to steal the county seat away from Peaceful Springs.

But Peaceful Springs had wasted little worry about it. It had been tried before and failed. It wasn't easy to get two thirds of the property owners of St. George County in the right mood to sign the petition to bring the issue to a vote. Nobody had expected the petition to get enough names this time, either.

But early in August there had been a concentrated drive in the city of Mapleton to get every property owner's signature. If they succeeded in that, they'd have well over half the signatures they needed. They wouldn't have to get many signatures from the west part of the county to force an election. A county-wide meeting had been held, and there was more sentiment favoring the move than anyone in Peaceful Springs had imagined. For the first time, alarm swept through the western half of the county.

When talk about countering the Mapleton drive arose, Troy found himself in the middle of it. He had too much to lose if the county seat was moved. His real estate business, the hotel and store that his father owned and were now his would all become almost worthless. He even doubted if his ranch would be worth as much if it were nearly thirty miles from the county seat instead of only a mile.

It had been a few years before that Jake Dett's wife had inherited a lot of money and Jake had bought a big ranch not far from Mapleton. Then he had come to Peaceful Springs and bought out two small neighbors of the Prescotts, one on either side of them. Immediately Jake Dett and all his money and greedy ambitions became a very vital problem for Troy and his father.

Jake Dett was not a man who could be crossed without retaliation. When he tried to buy out Frank Prescott, he was refused, and an undeclared war was begun. It appeared now that Jake Dett had won the war.

Troy managed to drop off to sleep eventually, but it was only to dream that he was facing Jake Dett in an arena, with only his hands for a weapon, while Jake had a long whip and a big knife.

The sun slanting against the bars on the south side of his cell roused Troy after a restless night. Today, if Mary and Doris could swing it, he would be released on bail.

But that dream was shattered before breakfast time

by a bull-throated voice roaring over by the court-house. Troy had heard that roar before and knew that trouble had arrived long before the judge opened his office, where his decision on bail would be announced.

Jake Dett must have ridden most of the night to be there this early. It would have taken the deputy until late last night to get word to him that Rafe had been killed. Troy wished he could see if Jake had brought his second son, Ike, with him. Ike was a huge man, just about Troy's age, who ramrodded Jake's ranch near Mapleton. His temper matched that of his father.

There was more yelling outside, and Troy realized that Jake was demanding that the sheriff open the jail so he could talk to the prisoner.

Troy heard footsteps outside, and then the door of the jail building was unlocked. The sheriff barely got inside before Dett shoved him to one side and strode toward the cells.

Jake Dett stood six feet two inches tall and weighed well over two hundred pounds. His brown hair was streaked with gray, but that didn't take away any of the strength and determination of the man.

"So you killed my son!" Jake stopped in front of Troy's cell, his legs spread apart, his fists clenched at his side. "Let me tell you something, Prescott! Take a good look at this sunrise. It's the last one you're ever going to see!"

3.

Troy glared back at Jake Dett without saying a word. Nobody ever won an argument of words with Jake.

The sheriff hurried over, stopping within five feet of Jake. "That's enough of that kind of talk," he snapped. "You said you had some civil questions to ask Troy. If you're only going to threaten him, you can get out right now."

"Who's going to put me out?" Jake demanded, glaring at the sheriff.

"I will if I have to," Hanson said, not flinching. Troy saw his hand on the butt of his gun.

Jake apparently saw that, too. He glowered at the officer for another minute, then wheeled back to Troy, ignoring Hanson.

"What made you think you could kill Rafe and get

31

away with it?"

"I didn't kill him," Troy said.

"He'll get a trial to decide whether he's guilty or not," the sheriff said.

Jake didn't even look at Hanson. "You won't ever come to trial," he said through gritted teeth, staring at Troy. "If they held the trial out here in this cow pasture, they'd get enough shirt-tail ranchers on the jury so they'd turn you loose. You ain't going to get that chance."

"That's enough, Jake!" Hanson repeated sharply. "Get out of here!"

Jake wheeled on the sheriff, but his belligerency faded when he saw that Hanson had drawn his gun.

"So you're taking his side, too," Jake said finally. "Pulling a gun on a decent citizen, while that murderer sits in there, as comfortable as a hen on a nest."

"I'm making sure you don't do something I'll have to hang you for," the sheriff said.

"That will be the day when you hang me!" Jake roared.

"You kill Troy, and I'll see that you do hang," Hanson said.

Troy admired the sheriff for his stand. Not many men would dare face Jake Dett and talk to him like that, even if he had a gun in his hand. But the combination of the gun and the badge apparently made

Jake reconsider any rash move.

Slowly he turned toward the outside door. "I can wait. But that scum is not going to go free after what he did."

Jake Dett went outside, and the sheriff followed him to the door and stopped there. After a while he shut the door and turned back to Troy.

"I never saw Jake any madder than he is now. He's always had his way. It's hard to say just what he'll do next."

"He practically told you," Troy said. "He aims to kill me some way before tomorrow morning."

Hanson nodded. "I'm going to move you over to a cell on the north side. He might try to sneak up to your cell and shoot you through the bars. Anybody in the courthouse can see what's going on outside your cell if you're on the north side."

Troy didn't object when the sheriff moved him to a cell across the runway. This cell had a north window. Through the bars, Troy could see the area between the jail and the big rock and brick courthouse, as well as the front yard east of the building. Anyone in the south half of the courthouse could see the north side of the jail.

Troy was astonished at the size of the crowd on the courthouse lawn. He quickly picked out Jake Dett and the even bigger frame of Ike Dett among those milling around in front of the courthouse. There were also many people from the Peaceful Springs area out there. Maybe they were just curious to see what Jake Dett was going to do. On the other hand, a lot of people who called themselves Troy's friends might be doubt-ful now. Murder, even the murder of an unlik-able man such as Rafe Dett, put an entirely dif-ferent veneer on friendship.

Troy could see that Jake Dett was talking earnestly to a half-dozen men around him. Troy didn't doubt that he believed that Troy had killed Rafe. There was no other suspect, and Troy had left himself open to charges when he had told the sheriff in the hearing of others that if the law didn't do something about Rafe, he would.

Troy switched his eyes to Ike Dett. Ike was ranting even louder than Jake. Closer to the jail but not making nearly so much racket was another Dett, Deek, Jake's oldest son. He was five inches shorter than his brother, Ike, and seventy-five pounds lighter. He had gone to college and become a lawyer. Jake had almost disowned him because he showed none of the love for the range and guns that his brothers did. But now Jake was probably glad to have Deek's legal help on the problems that kept arising.

Then Troy discovered another Dett whom he hadn't expected to see over there. Libby Dett was the only girl

34

among the Dett children. She was also the youngest, barely twenty now. She had another distinction in Troy's eyes. She was the prettiest girl he had ever seen. Even though he had crossed swords with her more than once, it hadn't changed his mind about her beauty.

Libby was small for a Dett, just the size of her mother, three inches over five feet tall and weighing only about a hundred and twenty pounds. She also had her mother's coal black eyes and hair. But in temperament, she was more like her father.

Troy saw Deek Dett motion his sister over to where he could talk to her. Troy disliked Deek as much as he did Jake or Ike. Deek was not the physical threat that Ike and Jake were, but he had a devious mind and would use it any way he could to gain his ends.

Troy grew tired of watching the milling crowd outside and lay down on his cot. He was almost asleep when the key rattled in the lock on the outside door and he sat up quickly. The sheriff swung the door open, then stepped back to let someone in ahead of him. Troy stared as he recognized Libby Dett.

"Just what are you looking for?" he asked a little gruffly.

Libby came down the alley between the cells and stopped in front of his. "I didn't come for a social visit," she snapped, her black eyes mirroring her anger. "Deek figured that Pa didn't give you a chance to say anything. He thought you might tell me something if I asked you instead of threatening you."

"If you think I'm going to admit I killed Rafe," Troy said carefully, "you're crazy."

"As members of Rafe's family, I think we have a right to know what happened."

Troy nodded. "As the man accused of killing him, I figure I've got the same right. But nobody has told me anything yet except that he was killed."

"You're lying," she said, her olive skin turning darker with fury. "There's nobody else who would have any reason to kill him."

"Reason or not, I didn't kill him," Troy said.

She gripped the bars so hard her knuckles turned white. "Rudy said you'd stick to that story but Deek thought you might give us a glimmer of the truth."

Troy wasn't surprised that Libby would admit she had listened to Rudy Yoeman. It was the talk of the whole county that Libby and Rudy Yoeman were practically engaged. He had come over to help Rafe run the Dett ranch just to get on better terms with the Dett family. But Troy saw something else that he had suspected.

"Deek must figure I still have a soft spot for you and that you could wind me around your finger," Troy said. "But I won't lie even to see you smile."

36

Troy thought for a moment that Libby was going to try to reach through the bars and scratch his eyes out. But she only stared at him, then wheeled toward the front door, where the sheriff obligingly let her out.

More of the natives of Peaceful Springs were leaving. Over half of the people still there were men who worked for Jake Dett. Troy noticed one man for the first time, although he was sure he must have been there all along. That was Norge Uldeen, Jake Dett's brother-in-law. His wife was the sister of Harriet Dett.

Norge Uldeen's wife, Hilda, was with him. She was larger than her sister, Harriet Dett, but she had the same jet black eyes and hair. And Troy had heard that she had much more of a temper than her sister had. She'd need it to live with Norge Uldeen. According to reports Troy had heard, he was as near nothing as was ever encased in a human skin.

Troy saw Mary Willouby and Doris Jewel coming across from the courthouse. They had Amos Brush, the local lawyer, with them.

The sheriff, who had taken up a permanent stand at the door of the jail, let the three inside. Troy was at the bars when they reached his cell.

"We won't be able to get you out of here until tomorrow morning," Mary said. "Mr. Brush talked to the judge. He set bail, all right, but it is mighty high."

"How high?" Troy asked.

37

"Ten thousand dollars."

Troy whistled. "It would take half the town to raise that much."

"Oh, we'll get it," Doris said confidently. "It's just a matter of it taking a little time. If the judge had been reasonable, we could have made it today."

"You've got lots of friends," Amos Brush said. "We'll get enough money and mortgages together to raise the bail before noon tomorrow."

"We need you out of here before we have our meeting to consider what to do about the petitions Mapleton is circulating," Mary said. "We don't want to see this thing come to a vote again."

Troy nodded. "I know what you mean. Their two thousand against our hundred. We'll have to get everybody who lives in the west half of the county to back us."

"Even that may not be enough," Mary said. "They need two thirds of the property owners to sign the petition, but only sixty percent of the votes at the election."

"I wish we could raise the bail tonight," Doris said. "I'd feel better with you out of here."

Troy glanced back at the barred window. "I've been in more comfortable places."

"Some of Jake Dett's men are downtown now," Amos Brush said. "But they aren't going home."

"Jake said I'd never see another sunrise," Troy said.

Mary looked back at the sheriff by the door. "Do you think he can hold them off?" she asked softly.

"That is what is worrying me," Brush said. "Wish you had some way of defending yourself if necessary."

"You're probably borrowing trouble," Troy said. "Jake Dett is a hothead, but he's no fool."

"I'm not so sure of that," Brush said. "Killing you is an obsession with him. Stay away from that window tonight."

"We'll get you out in the morning," Mary promised as they left the jail.

4.

The sun settled into the prairie, throwing its last shadow of the big courthouse across the creek and over the town to the east. Troy wondered if he was going to get any supper. The sheriff was still sitting on the chair he had carried to a spot just inside the front door of the jail.

Troy was looking his way when he saw him get up and knew someone was coming. He gripped the bars and waited. Then he heard Morrie Grote's voice at the door.

"Visitors," the sheriff announced as he let Morrie and a young black man about Morrie's age come in.

"You know Willie Ellis, don't you?" Morrie asked, bringing his friend to the cell bars.

Troy nodded. "Sure. From down near Elkhorn, aren't you?"

Willie grinned. "Yep. I came over this afternoon

and found that Morrie needed a little help."

"Doing what?" Troy asked.

"We've got troubles, Troy," Morrie said. "We were downtown looking for something to keep ourselves from starving to death and I heard some of Jake Dett's men talking. They're planning to break you out of here. You know what that means. A tall tree and a short rope."

Troy nodded. "I'm not surprised. But I don't know what anybody can do about it."

"We're hankering to try," Willie said.

"We'll talk to the sheriff first," Morrie said. "If he won't do anything, then we'll do what we can. Jake brought over most of the men who work for him."

"I saw that this afternoon," Troy said.

"We got to get our shirt-tails cracking," Willie said to Morrie. "These boys didn't say just when they plan to do this. Could be pretty quick."

Morrie nodded and turned back to the door. The sheriff opened it for them. "Got enough men to keep Jake from breaking into the jail?" Morrie asked the sheriff.

"I don't figure Jake is a lyncher," Sheriff Hanson said. "He's got a wild temper and he spouts off a lot. But when it comes right down to dragging a man out of jail and hanging him, I reckon that's beyond him."

"You sure are slow to catch onto things," Morrie said. "He's fixing to do just what you say he won't."

"Don't you try doing something to Jake," the sheriff warned. "That could upset the whole beehive."

"There's worse things than getting stung," Willie said as he and Morrie went outside and headed east.

It was the middle of the next morning when Amos Brush came to the jail again. Mary and Doris were with him. The sheriff let them inside the jail.

"I supposed you had work to do in the courthouse," Troy said to Mary.

"I've got more important business at the jail this morning," she shot back. "When you have a friend who is a jailbird—"

There was no levity in the lawyer. "We got your bail raised," he said. "As soon as the sheriff unlocks the door, you're a free man."

The sheriff was already turning the lock in the cell door. "Don't forget how this is going to strike the Detts," he warned Troy. "Having you out of this jail may be just what they are looking for."

"I'll be mighty careful," Troy promised. "Have they gone back to Mapleton?"

The sheriff nodded. "The whole kit and caboodle of them. But they won't stay there. They've got a ranch over here to take care of, you know."

"Now don't you skip out of the country," Brush said. "A good many of your neighbors helped raise this bail for you. If you disappear, it will be hard on them."

"I'm not running," Troy said. "You know me better than that."

Troy stepped out into the sunlight for the first time in over forty hours. He hadn't realized before how wonderful it was to be free to go where he wanted to.

"I'm not sure it's a good idea to let you run free," the sheriff said dubiously, following them outside the jail.

"Don't tell me you think he's guilty," Mary said sharply.

"It ain't that," Hanson said. "But Jake and Ike Dett may find it easier to kill him now than when he was in jail."

"Where will you stay, Troy?" Doris asked.

"I've got to go through Pa's papers out at the ranch," Troy said. "I have to find out how he was running things."

"You be careful," Mary warned. "And don't forget that tonight is the meeting at my place. We've got to do something about these petitions."

"Better tell him what we heard Betsy say," Doris suggested.

Troy shot a sharp look at Mary. "What about Betsy?"

"Maybe it's just a rumor," Mary said. "But we heard that she told somebody she knew that Rafe didn't kill your pa because she saw him somewhere else at that time."

"It had to be Rafe," Troy said. "But I'll talk to her."

He got his horse at the barn where the sheriff had put him after jailing Troy two days before. Since it was almost noon, anyway, he rode down to the hotel for dinner. There were only two others there for the meal, so Al and Emma Theim and Betsy ate with the customers.

Betsy gasped in surprise when she came from the kitchen and saw Troy among those waiting for dinner. "I knew the sheriff couldn't hold you on the evidence he had," she said.

"I heard that you don't think Rafe killed Pa," Troy said, finding a seat beside Betsy.

Betsy shot a look at her parents at the end of the table nearest the kitchen. "I'll tell you about that later," she said softly.

Troy nodded silently. He had gotten the feeling before that Betsy had several secrets from her parents.

After the meal, Troy went out to his horse, and Betsy followed.

"They had a celebration up at Tower that day, remember?" Betsy said when she reached the hitch-rack. "I went up there, but I didn't tell Pa or Ma that I was going. I saw Rafe Dett there, so I know he couldn't have been down here where they say he killed your pa. I don't want Pa to find out I was up at Tower."

44

"I'll pick you up tonight for the meeting at Mary's," he said, swinging into the saddle.

Betsy nodded, a sparkle coming into her eyes at last. "Maybe the meeting won't last too long. We can have some time alone."

Troy grinned. "We'll make sure of that."

Troy found Morrie at the ranch, and Morrie stayed with him like a burr through the afternoon as he rode over the ranch, checking cattle and fences. He wanted to get back to those papers in the safe, but he decided he'd have to wait until tomorrow to do that.

He went back to the hotel for supper before taking Betsy to Mary's for the meeting. Vivian Hurley, the dressmaker who had moved there from Mapleton not long ago, was already at Mary's. Troy was surprised. He hadn't expected her to favor keeping the county seat in Peaceful Springs.

Mary apparently saw the surprise on Troy's face. "Vivian came tonight because she has something important to tell us."

Troy looked around. Most of those he had expected had already arrived.

"What is so important?" he asked.

"Go ahead and tell him, Vivian," Mary said. "Tell everybody. We're all here now."

"Of course, you know I came here from Mapleton," Vivian said. "I guess the people there think I should still favor moving the county seat to Mapleton. They brought around a petition for me to sign to bring the issue to a vote. Now that I'm living here, I'd like to see the county seat stay here. It would be good for my business."

"Glad to have you on our side," Doris said.

"The reason I wanted to come to this meeting was to tell you what I saw on that petition. I didn't sign it, but I looked it over carefully. Several people have signed it who I am sure are not in favor of moving the county seat. But the petition peddlers have talked them into signing. I think we've got a better chance of winning this thing by keeping them from getting enough names on the petition than we have at the polls."

"That's right," Mary agreed. "They have to get two thirds of the property owners to sign the petition. They need only sixty percent of the votes to win the election."

"Why would anybody sign the petition if he is opposed to moving the courthouse?" the mayor of Peaceful Springs, Lew Arnett, asked.

"Their argument is that everybody should get a chance to have his say, so there should be an election," Vivian said. "They tried that on me, but I didn't fall for it."

Troy realized that they could lose the battle for the county seat right now during the petition drive.

5.

Troy looked around the ring of faces, most of them void of ideas. It was Doris who offered a suggestion.

"We'll have to get up a counter petition," she said. "We'll find out who around here has signed the Mapleton petition, and we'll get them to sign this one, taking their names off the other one."

"When Mapleton presents their petitions to the county commissioners to call for a special election," Mary added, "we'll be there with our petition and get those names off the list."

"We don't have much time," the mayor said. "The commissioners meet next Tuesday. Mapleton will probably present their petitions that day. This is Thursday."

"We'll start out tomorrow morning," Mary said. "Can you remember the names, Vivian?"

47

"Some," Vivian said. "I can get another look at that petition. They haven't given up on getting my signature."

"Good," Mary said, taking command of the situation as Troy had seen her do so often. "You give us the names you can remember now. We'll see those people tomorrow. Then when you get the names of other local people, give them to us. Nobody who lives in Peaceful Springs or west of here should want the county seat moved off to the northeast corner of the county. So we'll see any local people on their list. Amos, will you make up a petition to take their names off the Mapleton petition?"

The lawyer nodded. "I'll have several copies ready by morning."

As Troy had expected, the business part of the meeting was soon over. Most of the people stayed around to talk afterward. But Troy and Betsy slipped out and walked toward the hotel where Troy had left his horse.

"I start working for Vivian tomorrow morning," Betsy said. "I got the job just today."

"That's a good break for us," Troy said. "The Mapleton people still think they can get Vivian to sign, so they'll be back to see her. Get a look at that list if you can. You know the names of people around here better than Vivian does."

48

"Do we have to talk about that crazy old petition?" Betsy pouted.

He grinned. "That wasn't exactly what we had in mind, was it?" He reached out an arm and snuggled her to him, and they walked slowly up the hill toward the hotel, making one shadow.

When Troy left the hotel to ride to the ranch for the night, he was met by Morrie only a hundred yards from the hotel.

"What's this?" Troy demanded. "A bodyguard?"

"Reckon that's as good a name as any," Morrie said. "The sheriff thinks you should be mighty careful. The Detts are dangerous."

"Hanson is right about that," Troy admitted. "But I hardly figure I need a bodyguard."

"You might not if you were staying in the hotel, but if you're going to stay out at the ranch, that's different."

Troy didn't really expect the Detts to bother him at the ranch, either. But Jake and Ike Dett had made it clear that they intended to see to it that Troy paid for Rafe's death. The only way Troy was going to calm the Detts and clear himself with the law was to find the real murderer. That wasn't going to be easy.

Nothing disturbed the peace of the night at the ranch, and Troy rode out shortly after dawn to the spot where Morrie had said Rafe Dett had been found dead. Morrie went along like an armed escort. He seemed to have undertaken the job of keeping Troy alive. Troy supposed he should appreciate that.

At the site, they dismounted, and Troy looked around carefully. There was nothing unusual about the place. It was on the Smoky Hill River, and there were plenty of places along the banks where a man could hide and wait in ambush. Troy couldn't blame the sheriff for suspecting him. He had threatened to take the law into his own hands if the sheriff didn't find the man who had killed Frank Prescott. Now the Detts were making the same threats if the law didn't mete out punishment to the man they thought had killed Rafe Dett. It was a vicious cycle, and Troy was caught in the middle.

"Doesn't look like we're going to find anything here," Morrie said. "Thought we might see where the man waited in ambush."

"May not have been an ambush," Troy said. "The sheriff said Rafe had powder burns on his shirt. He was shot at close range. Maybe we're looking for the wrong thing. We'll have to think about it. I promised Mary I'd help get some of those signatures on our petition this afternoon. Let's go to the hotel for dinner."

"Couldn't be that the meals are better at the hotel with a certain girl doing the serving?" Morrie asked, grinning.

Troy shook his head. "She won't be serving today. She's got a job at Vivian Hurley's dress shop. Al and Emma don't need Betsy, with the little work that they have at the hotel."

As they rode into town, Morrie said thoughtfully, "I don't reckon we have anything to worry about today. The Detts are probably busy with Rafe's funeral. They said they were going to have it today."

Troy nodded. The undertaker from Mapleton had taken the body over yesterday, and the funeral was scheduled for this morning.

"They could be back here by this evening," he said.

Mary and Doris were waiting for them, and Mary had a list of names that Vivian had given her.

"These are the ones she remembers who live in the western half of the county," Mary said. "I can't believe they want the county seat moved. We'll check with them and explain the importance of getting their names off that petition if they don't want the county seat moved."

Troy and Morrie took three of the names of people who lived well out in the country. Mary gave them a copy of the petition Amos Brush had written. It would require plenty of riding to get to all three people and back before night.

Troy was disappointed when he found only one man home at the three places. This man listened carefully as Troy explained the situation and asked him if he'd sign the petition to take his name off the Mapleton list.

"I sure will," he said. "They told me they thought it was only fair that the whole thing be brought to a vote where everybody had a chance to have his say about it. That sounded reasonable, so I signed it. They said the petition itself wouldn't have anything to do with whether the county seat stayed in Peaceful Springs or not. I figured on voting against the move. Sure wish I hadn't signed their confounded petition."

He signed the petition Troy was carrying, which declared that the signers wished to have their names removed from the Mapleton petition. The date of this signing would be later than the one on the Mapleton petition.

When Troy and Morrie got back to Peaceful Springs, they found Mary and Doris disappointed in their afternoon's work.

"Almost everybody was gone," Mary said. "Now that doesn't make sense. Ordinarily, nobody goes anywhere on Friday afternoon. We had ten names on our list. We found only three at home. They all signed. They'd been hoodwinked into thinking that signing the Mapleton petition wouldn't do any harm."

"Seems strange so many were gone," Troy said. "Could it be they'd been coaxed away from home today by somebody who knew we were going to be looking for them?"

"I'm sure of it," Doris said. "And I've got an idea who."

Troy looked at Doris. "Who?"

"Libby Dett. She is a very good friend of Vivian's. She was in Vivian's shop yesterday morning before we got you out of jail. I'll bet the Detts gave those people enough money to go visit some relatives. They may not be back until after the petitions are turned in to the commissioners."

"Maybe we should talk to Vivian about it," Troy said.

Mary nodded. "I think so. Why didn't you tell me before what you suspected, Doris?"

"Just thought of it a while ago," Doris said. "I've been running it through my mind to see if it added up. It does, except that Vivian didn't know then that we were going to circulate these counter petitions. But she knew we were talking about doing something."

They started toward Vivian's dress shop. It was almost closing time, but they expected to find her there yet.

"By the way, Troy," Mary said as they moved along the street, "I heard something a while ago that should interest you. Norge Uldeen and his wife are going to move onto the ranch that Rafe Dett was running."

53

"Uldeen?" Troy repeated. "I guess I should have thought of that. He's Jake Dett's brother-in-law."

"Libby is coming over, too," Mary added. "I'm guessing she'll be the real boss. She is a Dett. And you know that Jake doesn't think much of his brother-in-law."

"Uldeen is a drunk," Morrie put in. "Can't blame Jake much for not trusting him with anything. I'll bet Libby will be the boss, all right."

"Rudy Yoeman is staying on, too," Doris said. "So you'll have four of the Dett faction as neighbors now instead of two, Troy."

"Uldeen and his wife will be no problem," Troy said. "Yoeman might be."

"Don't ever underestimate Libby," Mary said.

"Nobody ever underestimates a Dett, male or female, and lives to brag about it," Troy said.

"Glad you understand that," Doris told him. "Libby is as strong-willed as any of them, even if she isn't so violent. And I'm not sure she isn't that, too."

They reached the dress shop and went in. Vivian was getting her hat preparatory to leaving the shop. Betsy had apparently left for the day, but Libby Dett was there. Troy was surprised. He hadn't expected Libby or the Uldeens to come over from Mapleton at least for a day or two. Mary, who could usually rise to any occasion, seemed almost speechless at the sight of Libby.

"I take it they have something to say to you in private, Vivian," Libby said icily. "I'll wait outside for you."

Libby brushed past those in the doorway and went outside. Troy's eyes were drawn to her like steel to a magnet. She was a Dett, trying to get him hanged for murder. But all he saw at the moment was the beauty of her silky black hair and her sparkling dark eyes.

"Did Libby say anything about stashing away the people who signed their petitions so we couldn't find them?" Mary asked the moment Libby was through the door.

"No," Vivian said. "Of course, she favors moving the county seat to Mapleton. But she didn't say anything about any tricks."

"Somebody must have found out we were trying to get our local people to take their names off the Mapleton petition," Mary said. "We didn't find many of them home today. And people don't ordinarily leave home like that."

"I don't know how they found out," Vivian said. "I certainly didn't tell any of the Mapleton people."

Troy turned and stepped outside. Libby was around by the side of the dress shop by her buggy. One glance revealed that she had it loaded with little things she had brought from Mapleton for use at the ranch at Peaceful Springs.

"I see you're moving," Troy said. "Heard you were going to live over here."

"You've got good ears," Libby said sarcastically. "Are you planning to kill me, too?"

Troy didn't consider that worth an answer. "I suppose you've been working hard for the election?"

"As a matter of fact, I have," Libby said. "And I intend to keep on doing it. This little flea-bitten fly speck of a town has no right to be the county seat."

"You'd even go so far as to get people to leave the country to keep them from removing their names from your petition?"

Libby pursed her lips. "So that's what's eating you." She laughed. "I hope they all disappear where you can't find them. But it really doesn't matter, you know. We've got enough names right now to guarantee that a special election will be called."

Morrie and Mary and Doris came out then, and Troy joined them. Vivian locked her shop door and went to the buggy where Libby waited. Apparently Libby was going to take Vivian out to the ranch with her.

Troy shrugged as he met the others. He was positive that Libby had been exaggerating when she had said they had plenty of signatures. If they did have, they wouldn't work so hard to retain the names of those they had hoodwinked into signing the petition.

"Think she's the one?" Mary asked.

"She's the logical one," Troy said. "But it looks like she just came from Mapleton."

"They must have guessed we'd do something," Doris said. "We didn't decide on these petitions ourselves until last night."

"We'll work tomorrow and Sunday," Mary said. "Maybe we can catch more people home then."

Going home with Morrie, Troy thought of his own plight. He couldn't afford to spend all his time getting signatures on these counter petitions. He had to find the killer of Rafe Dett; it was the only way he was going to clear himself. Betsy's declaration that she had seen Rafe at Tower that day shook Troy's theory that Rafe had killed his father. But if not Rafe, then who? But proving or disproving that would have to wait until he had cleared himself of the charge of killing Rafe.

"Are you going to open your real estate office any more?" Morrie asked.

"Maybe," Troy said. "But nobody is going to be very interested in real estate until it is settled that the county seat is going to stay here."

They had better luck finding people at home on Saturday and at church on Sunday. But none of those missing on Friday were at home yet. Troy knew that was no accident. Still, when they totaled their lists

Sunday evening, they found that they would be able to take several names off the Mapleton petitions.

By noon on Monday they had checked every house in the area where someone lived who had signed the Mapleton petition.

"You've got a good safe at your ranch, Troy," Mary said. "Put these petitions there. No one will ever suspect that you have them."

Troy agreed and took all the petitions and headed home with Morrie. When they rode into the yard, they saw Willie lounging on the porch, his horse tied at the rack.

"Looks like you came to stay awhile," Morrie said, nodding at the stuffed gunny sack beside Willie.

"Yep. Got George to take care of my chores. Figured there ought to be two of us watching Troy. You can bet there will be more than two of them trying to kill him. I stopped down at the place where Rafe was killed. Saw something there I think you'll want to look at."

Troy took the petitions inside the house and laid them in the safe. He closed the door and hurried outside. The three rode down to the site, and Willie pointed out some odd hoofprints thirty yards upstream from the site of the killing.

Troy studied the prints for some time. One corner of the hoof was broken off. It was close to the water but far enough back so that it hadn't been washed out, although it was several days old. It could have been made by any rider passing along, but it was also possible that it had been made by the killer waiting for Rafe.

Troy thanked Willie for pointing it out, and they rode back to the ranch. When Troy reached the door, he stopped, his hand dropping to his gun. Someone had been there. If Troy had been home, he'd probably be dead now. His visitor might still be waiting for him inside.

6.

"What happened here?" Morrie demanded at Troy's elbow.

"Somebody paid us a visit while we were down at the river," Troy said, stepping inside and looking at the papers scattered over the room.

"They may still be around," Willie said softly, his eyes whipping over the room, then wheeling around to the yard.

"You check outside, Willie," Morrie said. "I'll look around in here."

"I'm going to see if they took anything," Troy said.

"Probably looking for you," Morrie said.

Willie pointed to the papers strewn over the floor. "Did they expect to find him under those?"

Willie went outside and moved cautiously around the house while Morrie crossed the room and pushed open the bedroom door. Troy began gathering up the papers, most of them unsorted mail that had come to Frank Prescott and had been stacked on one corner of the table.

Then Troy noticed that the safe door was open a crack. Reaching for it, he pulled it open. Only then did he remember that, in his haste to see what Willie had found down by the river, he had failed to lock the safe when he closed the door.

Hunching down, he looked inside. There was an empty space where he had laid the petitions. Quickly he opened the little drawer in the safe that held his father's important papers. Nothing in the drawer appeared to have been disturbed. It must have been the petitions that the burglar had wanted. They seemed to be all that was missing. He dreaded telling Mary and Doris that he had lost the petitions because he had carelessly forgotten to lock the safe.

Morrie came back from searching through the rest of the house. "Nobody in there," he said. "Doesn't even look like anybody has been in there."

"I think whoever it was found what he wanted right here," Troy said. "The petitions are gone."

Morrie nodded. "If they'd trick people into signing their petition when they knew they didn't want to move the county seat, they wouldn't hesitate to steal the petitions to take those names off." He looked at the unlocked safe. "Did they break in?"

"Forgot to lock it," Troy admitted. "I just closed the door."

"I'll bet they'd have ventilated you if you'd been here. Must have been some of the Detts."

"Let's go to town and tell Mary and Doris," Troy said.

They went for their horses, and Willie joined them. "They left their horses behind the barn," Willie reported. "But they were gone when we got here."

At Mary's, Troy dismounted and went to the door, while Morrie and Willie stayed with the horses. Mary answered Troy's knock. Doris was over at the school building. Even though it was Labor Day, this was the first day of the new school term, not a holiday.

Quickly Troy told Mary what had happened and ended by guessing that it must have been some of the Detts.

"Sounds logical," Mary agreed. "Let's talk to Amos. He can tell us how serious the loss of these petitions is."

They went to Amos Brush's home, because he had closed his office for the holiday. Mary explained what had happened.

"How much will this hurt us?" she asked.

Brush shook his head. "Plenty, I'm afraid. If they weren't worried about having enough signatures, they wouldn't have stolen our petitions."

"Then we'll just have to get those petitions back," Troy said. "The commissioners meet tomorrow. We'll have our petitions there."

"Any idea who took them?" Brush asked.

"Troy thinks it was the Detts," Mary said.

"I'm not sure they were after the petitions when they raided my place," Troy said. "They were probably looking for me. But they found the petitions. Have you seen Jake or Ike over here today?"

Brush shook his head. "No. But I haven't been in my office, so I don't know who has been in town."

"I'll check with Al Theim," Troy said. "He sees about everybody who comes to town."

Mary went with him to the hotel. Al Theim shook his head when asked if he had seen any of the Detts.

"Only Dett I've seen in town was Libby," he said. "And she was here only a few minutes."

"I can't quite picture Libby as a thief," Mary said as they left the hotel.

"I can if it would help move the county seat," Troy said. "It must be somebody from that ranch. I don't think Norge Uldeen has nerve enough to break into anybody's house. But there is Rudy Yoeman. I wouldn't put anything past him."

"Neither would I," Mary said. "Yoeman could have come up there with the intention of killing you. He'd do anything to get in good with the Detts."

"And nothing would put him in solider with them than killing me," Troy agreed. "We've got to have those petitions back. I'm going down there and have a look."

"That's like walking up the gallow steps and putting the noose around your own neck," Mary said. "Better let Morrie do it. They wouldn't kill him if they caught him."

"It's my fault those petitions are gone," Troy said. "I won't ask Morrie to do it."

They went back to Amos Brush's house, where Troy had left his horse. Morrie and Willie were still in town, and Troy doubted if they had ever lost sight of him as he moved around town with Mary. Now as he mounted, he saw the two get their horses down by the store and come to meet him.

Troy considered ways of slipping away from Morrie and Willie to go to the Dett ranch. If Rudy Yoeman had taken the petitions, that was where they would be. But if he mentioned what he had in mind, Morrie would never let him go; at least not alone. And it was not Morrie's risk to take.

Back at the ranch, Morrie outlined the way he intended to guard Troy. "We haven't used the old bunkhouse for a couple of years, but Willie is going to sleep out there. I'll bunk on the couch in the front room of the house. Nobody is going to slip in on us unexpectedly."

Troy nodded as though he were in agreement. He expressed weariness as soon as supper was over. Then he wrote a note to Mary and asked Willie if he would take it to her.

Willie agreed, then looked at Morrie. "Go ahead," Morrie said. "I'll keep an eye on things here. Just don't be gone any longer than you have to be."

"I'll deliver the note and come right back," Willie said. "Want me to wait for an answer, Troy?"

Troy shook his head. "That won't be necessary. I just forgot to tell her something."

He sealed the envelope and handed it to Willie. If Willie realized that the note merely told Mary that he was going to try to get the petitions back, he wouldn't take it to town.

As soon as Willie left for town, Troy yawned and stretched and told Morrie he was going to bed. He left Morrie in the front room, arranging some blankets on the couch for his own bed.

As soon as Troy got to his room, he opened the window, ignoring the squeal it made. Morrie would only think he was opening the window to get some air. Quietly he climbed through the window and hurried to the corral. The horses knew him and made no commotion. Within five minutes after leaving Morrie,

Troy was leading his horse quietly away from the corral.

A hundred yards from the barn, he mounted and kept his horse at a walk as he headed for the Dett ranch, only about a mile away. He crossed the river and finally reined up in some scrubby trees a hundred yards from the house. Lights were still burning in the house.

Moving quietly forward on foot, he got as close as he thought he dared and crouched where he could see the house and the yard. If he barged in, he'd have to depend on the advantage of complete surprise. Somebody was in the yard at the moment, and he strained his eyes to see who it was. Then the door opened, and Libby was outlined in the light streaming from inside. He heard Rudy Yoeman call to her that he had the buggy ready. Libby stepped outside and closed the door.

Obviously Rudy Yoeman was taking Libby for an evening buggy ride. That left only Norge Uldeen and his wife, Hilda, in the house and greatly reduced the danger when Troy charged in. But it also reduced his chances of success. The Uldeens might not know where Yoeman had put the petitions.

He had started toward the house when the light went out inside. That changed his strategy. Maybe he could slip in, find the petitions and slip out again without being detected. That would be safer. So he settled down to give Norge and Hilda Uldeen time to get to sleep.

After waiting fifteen minutes, Troy moved silently to the door. Quietly he tried the doorknob. He didn't expect it to be locked, not with Libby and Rudy Yoeman still out. The door opened without a squeal, and Troy stepped inside.

He had been in the house many times when the Johnsons owned it. If the new owners hadn't rearranged things, he could go directly to the little room that Hiram Johnson had used for an office. That seemed like the logical place for the petitions to be.

He moved on tiptoe across to the inner room, his eyes, accustomed to the dark, barely making out a big chair in his path in time to avoid it. Once inside the little room, he pushed the door shut, then struck a match. Practically nothing had been changed.

Quickly he went to the desk and looked at the papers there, but the petitions were not on top. The match burned down to his fingers, and he had to blow it out and strike another one. He began pulling out the drawers. Maybe he had gussed wrong; maybe neither Yoeman nor Libby had taken the petitions. Or maybe they had sent them directly to Jake Dett.

Then, in the third drawer, he found them, lying on top of some other papers. He wasn't surprised that they were on top. Certainly neither Yoeman nor Libby would expect anyone to come snooping in there looking for them. He wondered why they hadn't burned them. In their place, he would have. But probably Rudy wanted to show them to Jake Dett to prove what he had done. Troy didn't doubt that the main goal in Rudy Yoeman's life was to work himself into the good graces of Jake Dett.

Folding the petitions and slipping them into his pocket, he turned back toward the door.

7.

Reaching his horse, Troy swung into the saddle and headed at a hard gallop back to his own ranch. When he rode up to the corral, he was immediately challenged by Willie, who stepped around the barn with a rifle in his hand. He stared in amazement when he recognized Troy.

"Morrie said you went to bed right after I took that message to Mary Willouby," he said.

"I went past the bed and out the window," Troy admitted. "I had to get those stolen petitions back, and I knew you two would tag along if you knew I was going. It was my job to get them; not yours."

"But it would have been just fine for you to get killed doing it," Willie snorted. "Is that it?"

Troy nodded. "Maybe that's one way of looking at it. Anyway, I've got the petitions."

Troy unsaddled his horse and went with Willie to the house. Morrie roused the instant the outside door opened. He was furious when he learned that he'd been tricked, but he held his temper in check.

Troy slept only fitfully. He expected Yoeman to do almost anything to get those petitions back. But when nothing happened, he decided that maybe Yoeman hadn't discovered that they were gone.

Morning came in complete serenity, and Troy hurried through breakfast to get to town with the petitions.

The commissioners met in the courtroom, the only room large enough to accommodate the crowd squeezing in to witness the proceedings. They went through their regular business, apparently reluctant to bring up the hot issue of the petitions to force a special election on the county seat. Finally they finished their other business, and the petitions were called for.

Troy sat with Mary and Amos Brush and waited. There was nothing for them to do until the petitions were acted upon. If the commissioners decided there were enough names on the petitions to force an election, then Amos Brush would challenge some of the names.

The commissioners went over the list deliberately checking it against the list of property owners they had been given. It seemed to Troy that they were deliberately wasting time. But there was nothing Amos Brush could do until the commissioners acted. Then, late in the afternoon, the commissioners recessed until nine o'clock the next morning.

"Now why did they do that?" Troy demanded as they left the meeting.

"So they wouldn't have to show us that list of names today," Brush said. "If we saw it now, we might still get some of the people to take their names off. In the morning, they'll present the list and take immediate action. My guess is that they have enough names but are afraid that we can successfully challenge too many. By waiting till morning to make the list public, they have stopped us from knowing whom else to reach to remove more names."

"I don't like the looks of it," Mary said.

"Can't say that I do, either," Brush agreed. "But there's nothing we can do. We must abide by the laws."

"No matter how they are manipulated," Mary added disgustedly.

Troy was back in the courtroom the next morning with Mary and Amos Brush. The petitions were taken up immediately, since there was no other business before the commissioners. The list was presented, and the commissioners announced that more than two thirds of the property owners in the county had signed the petition. Amos Brush was on his feet instantly and challenged the accuracy of the list. He demanded to see the list, and it was handed over to him.

Brush glanced down the list, then picked up his own petition. The commissioner from the east end of the county squirmed uncomfortably as Brush stepped forward.

"There are several names on this petition that I challenge," Brush said. "We have petitions here, signed by certain people, requesting that their names be removed from the original petition. Each signature is dated later than the corresponding signature on the original petition."

Brush handed the petitions to the commissioners. They looked at the names and nodded.

"We'll have to go over this list carefully and strike the names of those who have requested removal," Ray Fly, the commissioner from the west end of the county, said. "It will take some time."

"I doubt if it will change anything," said Oliver Tingley, another commissioner. "The petition we have already considered has more than enough names to call for an election."

"I'd like to see that corrected list myself before you make your final decision," Brush said.

"We'll give you that privilege," agreed Jim Older, the third commissioner.

Troy went to his real estate office for a while during the middle of the day when it became obvious that the commissioners were going to stall a decision as long as possible. There was practically no activity in land buying now. Everyone seemed to be waiting to find out if there was going to be a special election on the county seat. If it was decided there would be an election, Troy knew that his real estate business would practically go into limbo until after the election.

Late in the afternoon, Troy went back to the courtroom and found Mary and Amos Brush still waiting. At five-thirty Oliver Tingley, as chairman of the commissioners, announced the decision of the board.

"According to the official list of property owners in this county," Tingley said, "there must be at least fourteen hundred and fifty-one signatures to constitute two thirds of the eligible petition signers. There are fifteen hundred and forty-two names on the original petition. The counter petitions have given cause to eliminate sixty-six of these names. The result is that we have fourteen hundred and eighty legitimate signatures. That is twenty-nine more than necessary to call a special election."

"We lost that round," Troy said dejectedly as they left the courthouse. "Since they got over two thirds of the property owners to sign that petition and they need only sixty percent of the voters to move the county seat, our chances in the election don't look good, either."

"There are a lot of people who signed that petition who won't vote for the move, though," Mary said confidently. "Didn't you see their petition? If we'd seen that yesterday, we could have gotten a hundred more names scratched off. They knew it, too. That's why the names weren't made public till this morning."

"We won't give up without a fight," Amos Brush said. "Mary's right. There are several whose names are on that petition who won't vote yes at the election."

"When will the election be?" Troy asked.

"This has to be a special election," Brush said. "It can't be held in conjunction with a general election. It must be held within fifty days of the decision to hold an election, and it has to be advertised at least thirty days in advance. So the date must be set soon. Fifty days from now will be about the twenty-seventh of October. So it will be before that, and it can't be less than thirty days after they announce the date. I'd guess it will be somewhere between the tenth and twenty-fifth of October."

"We'll have plenty of work to do between now and then," Mary said.

"My trial will come up this fall, too," Troy said.

"When will that be?"

"The fall term of court in St. George County will be the second week in November," Amos Brush said. "We must find some evidence of your innocence before then, or we may be in serious trouble."

"What can we do?" Troy asked.

"Hopefully, find the man who did kill Rafe Dett," Brush said. "Barring that, dig up some proof that you weren't near the murder site at the time of the killing. All their evidence is circumstantial, but it is damaging. You have a good reputation, and we will rely heavily on that. But that may not be enough."

"I'll find something if it is to be found," Troy promised.

Troy went to his horse and met Morrie there. Together they rode the mile down to the ranch on Smoky Hill.

The next morning Troy and Morrie searched the area where Rafe Dett had been killed, but they didn't find anything new. Willie stayed at the ranch, because he and Morrie had decided that someone should stay close after what had happened the other day when they had all been gone.

Willie rode into town with Troy after dinner. They found Mary and Amos Brush at the courthouse, poring over the precinct voting records.

"I thought you checked those before the commissioners' meeting," Troy said.

"Those were the property owners who could sign the petition," Mary said. "Anybody of legal age and residency can vote in the election, whether he owns property or not."

"It's to our advantage to get every legal voter on the list," Brush said. "For instance, there are some men in the army now. Their names are to be counted, since this county is their legal residence, even if they are in Cuba or the Philippines. Every name like that will be the same as a No vote in the election."

"Don't forget the people down around Elkhorn," Willie said.

"We won't forget them," Mary promised. "Are there some there who have never voted who are eligible to vote?"

"I reckon there may be," Willie said. "Some of my people still remember being slaves, and they're not too anxious to follow the white man's rules, even when it comes to voting."

"How do they feel about moving the county seat?"

Willie shrugged. "Some may vote for the move. But a lot of the older people don't want to make any change. They've got things better now than they've ever had them before, and they don't want to risk any change that might make things worse."

"We must make sure everyone down there who is of

legal voting age is counted," Mary said. "And we want to get them to vote against moving the county seat. You can help us there, Willie."

"I'll do what I can," Willie promised.

An hour after Troy and Willie arrived, a half-dozen people from Mapletown came into the clerk's office. Immediately Troy felt the tension rise. They let it be known they were there to check the voting list, too. But they were looking for names that could be eliminated, such as those who had died or moved out of the county.

Not a word was exchanged between the two groups. It was Willie's sudden entrance that broke the tension for Troy. Willie had been out on the east steps on the courthouse, watching for trouble. Now he hurried over to the spot where Troy was working with Mary and Amos Brush.

"Jake and Ike Dett just rode up," Willie whispered. "I figure it's time for you and me to make ourselves hard to find."

"I'm not going to run," Troy said.

Mary pushed him toward a side door. "A live coward is worth a lot more to us than a dead hero."

Troy still hesitated, knowing that his stubbornness could cost him his life.

8.

Sheriff Hanson came hurrying into the room, his eyes flashing over the people half filling the clerk's office. When his eyes stopped on Troy, he plowed through to him.

"Come on, Troy," he said, taking his arm. "Jake and Ike are outside. I want you out of here before they come in."

"Why should I run?" Troy demanded.

"To avoid trouble," the sheriff said angrily. "It was only last week that Rafe was killed."

"I don't have to run from anybody," Troy said stubbornly. "If Jake and Ike try to make trouble, it is your job to stop it."

The sheriff swore softly. "That's what I'm trying to do by getting you out of here. There won't be any trouble if they don't see you."

"They're going to see me sometime," Troy said. "It might as well be now."

The sheriff swore again, then turned toward the door in an apparent attempt to keep the Detts from coming in. But he was too late. Jake and Ike Dett stepped through the door before the sheriff got there.

Jake stopped, spraddle-legged, and surveyed the room, obviously astonished by the number of people he saw. He saw Troy first, but there was little change in his expression. His small eyes squeezed a bit narrower, but he said nothing. Ike, on the other hand, dropped into a crouch when he saw Troy, his hand touching the butt of his gun. Troy wore his gun only when he expected trouble, and he hadn't expected it this afternoon.

"Watch it, Ike," Sheriff Hanson warned. "There are a lot of people here, and Troy isn't armed."

"That's his tough luck," Ike said through set teeth.

"It might be yours, too," Hanson said.

Ike didn't take his eyes off Troy, but Jake reached over, got a grip on Ike's shoulder, and his fingers dug in. Ike flinched.

"Calm down, Ike," Jake said sharply. "There are too many people here. Besides, he'll be coming to trial soon. He won't go free. I'll guarantee that."

Ike shrugged out of his father's grip. He still glared at Troy, but his hand moved away from his gun.

"There'll be a better time," he said. "But I ain't trusting the law to do the job."

"You go easy on those threats," Hanson said. "Threats are what put Troy where he is now."

"He carried out his threats," Ike said. "I figure on doing the same."

Jake wheeled Ike toward the door and pushed him outside. Troy found it hard to relax for a few minutes. It had been closer than he had thought it would be. Ike had almost killed him. The number of witnesses and Jake's hard hand had kept him from it.

Doris came as soon as school was dismissed, and they made faster progress, thanks to her keen eyes and quick hands. Still the job wasn't completed when it came time to close the office for the day.

"We've got plenty of time," Mary said. "The commissioners haven't even set the day for the election yet."

Outside, Troy found Willie waiting on the steps, where he had kept an eye on Ike and Jake Dett as long as they stayed near the courthouse.

"Have they gone home?" Mary asked anxiously.

"I think so," Willie said.

You be careful, Troy," Mary said, touching his arm. "Don't take Ike's threats lightly."

"I'm not liable to," Troy said. "But Jake seems willing to wait for the trial. Maybe he'll keep Ike in line."

"Only while they're together," Mary said. "When Ike gets away from Jake, there's no telling what he might do. Maybe you should stay at the hotel."

Troy shook his head. "I don't want to leave the ranch. They might burn the buildings."

"With you in them," Doris added.

"Not likely, while I've got two watch dogs keeping an eye on things," Troy said. "Morrie is out there today to make sure nothing happens to the ranch."

"We try to keep him in sight all the time," Willie said. "But it ain't easy."

As Troy and Willie headed southeast toward the ranch, Willie added to his earlier warning.

"I heard a couple of fellows talking to Ike after Ike left the courthouse," he said. "They're fixing to do something. I couldn't understand what it was, but we've got to watch out for them."

"Maybe we'll just stick around the ranch for a few days," Troy said. "There is a lot of work to do, anyway."

"I ain't sure the ranch is the safest place in the world for you," Willie said dubiously. "Ike knows you're staying there. He wasn't just barking at the moon today when he said he was going to get you. He aims to do it."

Troy unsaddled his horse and turned him into the corral. Morrie reported that everything had been quiet at the ranch.

Mary and Doris drove out in Mary's buggy after school hours the next evening. It was Monday, and Mary had come to tell Troy that the commissioners had set October 18 as the day for the special election to decide whether the county seat would be moved to Mapleton.

"We must get started immediately on our campaign to get people to vote for Peaceful Springs," Mary said. "The election is just five weeks from tomorrow. We'll need your help."

"I heard some youngsters at school today talking about a meeting at Uldeen's tonight," Doris added. "Their folks had been invited. Most weren't going. But the Frisbee boy said his pa was going. You can bet that's a meeting aimed at getting people over here to vote for Mapleton."

Troy rubbed his chin. "I'd sure like to know who goes to that meeting and what they talk about."

"I don't think many people from this end of the county will support Mapleton," Mary said. "We're going to have a rally in Peaceful Springs soon. We'll need you to help us plan that."

Troy agreed, and Mary and Doris drove back toward town.

Troy took a bath and put on fresh clothes before heading toward the corral to saddle his horse. Morrie and Willie intercepted him, arguing that he should not be riding out after nightfall. Troy agreed to let Morrie go with him.

They saw a couple of wagons in front of the house, plus three saddled horses. Apparently only a few neighbors had accepted the invitation to the meeting.

"Let's see if we can find out what they're saying," Troy said softly. "The Uldeens don't have a dog."

They moved quietly up to the house and around close to a window. Troy peeked inside. He saw only two of his neighbors, John Frisbee and Marc Siddon. The saddled horses apparently belonged to Ike Dett and two of the Dett riders from over near Mapleton.

Ike Dett seemed to be in charge of the meeting, but he wasn't shouting as he usually was, and his voice was muffled by the closed window. Troy found it hard to make out anything he was saying. He was sure he heard the word courthouse several times, but he couldn't hear enough to make an intelligent guess as to what was being said about the courthouse.

Then one of Ike's men got up and headed for the door. Troy grabbed Morrie's arm, and they slipped back into the shadows. The man came outside, leaned against the wall near the door and rolled a cigarette.

"They must have decided to put out a guard," Troy whispered after a while. "We might as well go home."

Carefully they moved back until they were far

enough away so that the guard at the door couldn't hear their movements; then they hurried to their horses and rode back toward Troy's ranch.

"They sure were talking a lot about the courthouse," Morrie said.

"I was thinking the same thing," Troy agreed.

"I'm sure I heard Ike say something about getting rid of it," Morrie said.

"Maybe we'd better think of some way to find out just what they were talking about."

Morrie nodded. "I agree. We'll have to worm it out of somebody who was at that meeting. But just who will that be?"

"There was only one there who might talk. That's Norge Uldeen. Especially if he gets drunk enough."

"He's always drunk," Morrie said. "But we'll have to pick our time and place. Can you imagine where we'd be now if Ike had caught us tonight?"

"Ready for the undertaker," Troy said. "We'll catch Uldeen alone sometime."

Troy went to town the next afternoon to meet with Mary and Doris and Amos Brush to make plans for the rally at Peaceful Springs. The meeting was set for four-fifteen so Doris could get there from school.

Morrie and Willie had come to town with Tony but had stayed at the store while Troy went to the meeting. The planning session for the rally was barely started when Morrie came to the door. Troy hurried outside.

"What's wrong?" he demanded.

"Something's right for a change," Morrie said with a grin. "Norge Uldeen just drove into town alone, and Willie is talking to him now—with a bottle."

"Getting him drunk?" Troy asked.

"Drunker than usual," Morrie corrected. "I thought you might want to be there when we get him to talking."

Troy nodded and called in to Mary and Doris that he had some business downtown that couldn't wait. Then he hurried off with Morrie. They found Willie and Norge Uldeen sitting on the long bench in front of the store. Willie kept offering Norge a bottle he periodically slipped out of his pocket, and Uldeen didn't refuse a single invitation.

"What was going on at that meeting I hear you had at your place?" Willie asked as Troy and Morrie came up.

Uldeen grinned knowingly. "Can't tell you," he mumbled. "Promised to keep it a secret."

"You can tell me," Willie coaxed. "Ain't I your buddy? If I'm not, I'm sure wasting my whiskey."

"You're my buddy, all right," Uldeen said hastily. "But I just can't tell you anything. Hilda would kill me. Or Libby would. Or Ike. Or Rudy. I just can't tell you."

Uldeen weaved uncertainly on the bench. "Remember, Norge," Willie said confidentially, "if you don't tell the truth, you're liable to wake up paralyzed one of these days. That's what happens to people who won't tell the truth."

Uldeen stared at Willie with wide eyes. "Is that a fact?" He reached for the bottle that Willie offered and took another long drink.

Troy didn't know Norge Uldeen very well, but he had heard that he passed out completely after too many drinks. He was on the verge of passing out now. Willie repeated his warning just as Norge toppled over on the bench.

Willie got up and walked off a way with Morrie and Troy. Troy looked back at Uldeen, out cold.

"What have you got in mind, Willie?" Troy asked.

"I hope he remembers what I said about waking up paralyzed sometime if he doesn't tell the truth," Willie said, "because he's going to wake up with his legs paralyzed this time."

"How are you going to manage that?" Morrie asked.

"With some broomsticks up his pants legs," Willie said with a big grin.

Troy chuckled and went with Morrie to find the broomsticks. They found at the livery barn one broom that was worn out, and the livery man was glad to give it to them. They found the other one at Mary's. Her broom wasn't completely worn out, but she sacrificed it for what she considered a good cause.

Troy found a saw and cut off the sweeping ends of the brooms, then took them back to Willie. He pushed the sticks inside Uldeen's pants legs till they reached from his hips to his boots.

Then it was a matter of waiting. Uldeen seldom stayed out too long, Troy had heard. But it was late evening this time before he roused and tried to sit up. When he swung his legs off the bench and found he couldn't bend them, he blinked, apparently too dazed to comprehend what was wrong. He stared at his legs in bewilderment.

Then suddenly fear welled up into his face. "Hey," he yelled, looking up at Willie, "I can't use my legs."

"I told you you'd wake up paralyzed some day if you didn't tell the truth," Willie said.

"I don't dare tell," Uldeen stammered. "They'd kill me."

"Just tell me what they're going to do to the courthouse," Willie insisted.

Fear widened Uldeen's eyes, and he shook his head. "They'd kill me!"

"Do you want to stay paralyzed the rest of your life?" Willie asked.

Uldeen heaved himself to his feet and tried to run.

The broomsticks kept his legs from bending, and he pitched headlong on the sidewalk, hitting his head on the post of the hitchrack at the edge of the sidewalk.

"Knocked himself out," Willie muttered. "Doesn't look like this is going to work. Let's get these sticks out of there. We may want to try something else on him sometime. If he gets wise to us now, nothing will work next time."

Troy agreed with that reasoning, and he and Willie took the broomsticks out of Uldeen's pants. As they left for home, Troy looked back once to see Uldeen sitting up, working his legs back and forth like a youngster who had just found a brand-new toy.

9.

The rally at Peaceful Springs was set for the next Tuesday. At the final planning meeting on Thursday, Troy voiced a new idea.

"Willie tells me that his people down around Elkhorn are undecided on where they want the county seat. Now if we could swing them over to our side, it might make a difference."

"It certainly would," Mary agreed. "Would Willie go down there with us to talk to them?"

"I'm sure he would."

"We'll go on Saturday," Mary decided. "Doris can go with us then."

Willie's face beamed when Troy told him their plans. He stuck close to Troy on Friday, as Troy tried to dig up some evidence that would help him when his trial came up. Amos Brush repeatedly told Troy to be patient and wait for a break. But it seemed to Troy that patience was a poor virtue, with the trial date coming up so rapidly.

Elkhorn was about twenty miles as the crow flies southeast of Peaceful Springs. Early Saturday morning, Troy went with Mary and Doris, while Willie rode on ahead to round up his family and neighbors.

Elkhorn was little more than a store and post office, but there were several wagons and quite a few people waiting when Troy stopped the spring wagon in front of the store. Troy and Mary did most of the talking. Willie added a little, and they listened more attentively to him than to Troy.

"Some want to know what the advantage is if they vote for Peaceful Springs?" Willie said during a lull in the talking and visiting.

"We can promise them a big celebration if we win," Troy said.

Willie grinned. "That may be enough. My folks love celebrations."

"Don't we all?" Troy said. "I heard one man say he knew some people who couldn't get to the polls. Maybe we can come down and take them."

"They'll appreciate favors like that," Willie said. "Might even guarantee their No vote on the move to Mapleton."

"Don't forget our rally Tuesday night at the

courthouse," Mary said as they drove back to Peaceful Springs.

"I'm not liable to forget that," Troy assured her.

Troy spent Sunday with Betsy. He picked her up and took her to church in the morning, ate dinner with her family at the hotel, then took her for a ride down to the ranch and back in the afternoon. Morrie was his shadow all day, but he kept his distance, so that Troy and Betsy had some degree of privacy.

Troy enjoyed the day, and Betsy bubbled like the springs just to the south of town. She made some fudge when they got back to the hotel, and Troy spent most of the evening there before heading back to the ranch with Betsy's promise to go to the rally with him Tuesday night.

He was at the hotel early Tuesday evening, and his eyes widened in appreciation as Betsy whirled into the room, showing off a new dress she had just made.

"If this was a dance, you'd be the belle of the ball," Troy said admiringly.

"I don't want you to be ashamed of me," Betsy said.

"Not much chance of that," Troy declared.

As they left the hotel, Al Theim called after them that he and Emma would be along later.

The rally was being held in the courtroom of the courthouse. The place was half full when Troy and Betsy got there. Mary and Doris were at the center of things, reviewing the order in which the speakers would take the stand and emphasizing the points they were to make.

Mary gave the first speech, a real pep talk, but before she could call Amos Brush to the podium, a murmur rippled through the crowd. Troy turned to see what had caused it. Rudy Yoeman and Norge Uldeen were standing in the opening of the double doors on the east side of the room. There could be only one reason for them to be there. They hoped that their presence would put a damper on the rally.

Troy soon discovered that Yoeman, at least, had more than that in mind. When Amos Brush began to talk, Yoeman stood up to interrupt and argue with him. Troy left his chair and moved toward Yoeman. He'd almost had a fight with him once or twice before. This time there wasn't likely to be anything to stop it.

But Troy hadn't figured on Betsy. She moved quickly past him and reached Rudy Yoeman before Troy did.

"Let's go for a walk, Rudy," she said softly.

Troy stopped dead in his tracks as he saw Rudy's belligerence wilt. "I didn't come here to walk around," he said, trying to sound rough.

"If you start trouble, I'll get this new dress all mussed up," Betsy said. "You wouldn't want that, would you?"

"You don't have to get mixed up in it."

"But I will," Betsy said. "I don't want any trouble here. Let's go outside and talk it over."

Troy was amazed to see Rudy nod and turn quietly toward the door with Betsy. He was anything but happy to have Betsy going outside with Rudy, but she had kept the rally from turning into a brawl.

Norge Uldeen stayed in his chair, but he twisted uncomfortably. He had come with Yoeman, more like a shadow than a visible force. But now there was nothing for the shadow to reflect. So he sat there, looking as unhappy as a fly in a spider web.

The meeting proceeded. Troy took his turn at the speaker's stand, urging a concentrated effort to get every vote possible for Peaceful Springs. But his mind was more on Rudy Yoeman and Betsy somewhere outside than it was on what he was saying.

As soon as the meeting was over, Troy hurried downstairs. He found Betsy and Rudy on the east steps of the courthouse, visiting like old friends. Troy was none too gentle in suggesting it was time he took Betsy home. Rudy bristled, but then he looked at Betsy and wilted again. Troy was amazed at the influence Betsy had over him.

Troy and Morrie rode back to town the next day, and Troy talked to Amos Brush about the coming trial. Brush had little to offer in the way of new evidence for the defense. But he didn't appear overly concerned. Justice would prevail, he insisted. Troy lacked Brush's confidence.

When they got home that afternoon, they found Willie excited. He came from the bunkhouse to meet Troy and Morrie at the barn.

"We've had visitors again," he said. "I saw them over on the knoll where those fellows showed up before. So I got back inside the bunkhouse and waited. After a while they rode into the yard and looked all around, but they didn't get off their horses."

"Did you recognize them?"

Willie shook his head. "No. But I figure they're some of Dett's men from the ranch over near Mapleton. He's not liable to send over the same men that got sent up here the other night."

"We'll keep a couple of horses saddled tonight," Morrie said. "If they decide to pay us a visit after dark, we'll be ready to ride out and nab them."

Troy kept on the alert that evening, watching with Morrie and Willie. Morrie stayed by the living room window, while Troy watched from the back of the house. Willie was in the bunkhouse, and he had his and Morrie's horses saddled and tied just behind the building.

A short while after dark, Morrie called softly to Troy. "Somebody is sneaking in from the east."

Since there was nothing stirring behind the house,

Troy left his post and hurried into the living room. The moon, only half full the other night, was bigger now, and it was a clear night. Troy followed Morrie's pointing fingers and saw two riders moving slowly down the slope toward the ranch.

"If they get a little closer, I might pick one off," Morrie said, fingering his rifle.

"Hold on," Troy said. "We don't know who they are. You wouldn't want to shoot a friend, would you?"

"Never saw a friend sneak in like that," Morrie grumbled. "I'm going to find out who they are and what they're up to. I'll go out the back door and over to the bunkhouse. Willie and I will surprise them."

Troy stayed by the window and watched the two visitors. They had stopped out beyond the corrals and seemed to be studying the place as if trying to decide whether it was safe to ride on in or not.

Suddenly Morrie and Willie exploded from behind the bunkhouse and charged toward the two riders out in the moonlight. They were twenty yards from the bunkhouse before the visitors spotted them. The intruders dug in their spurs and galloped up the slope and out of sight, Morrie and Willie in hot pursuit.

Troy watched them go over the hill, then settled down to wait for their return. He wondered if it could be a trap. The two riders might have been decoys to lure Troy and his men away from the ranch, where more men waited in ambush.

But Troy heard no gunfire. In fact, the night was so still that it was eerie. There was no movement anywhere in the yard, and Troy got up and wandered to the rear of the house.

Alarm suddenly electrified him as he stepped into his bedroom. Smoke was curling up through the open window. Running across the room, he poked his head outside. Fire was lapping up the side of the building.

It flashed through his mind that they had been outmaneuvered. Those riders out on the hill had been decoys. While Morrie and Willie had chased them, other men had slipped in and set fire to the house. Since Troy hadn't gone with his hired men, they had set the fire at his bedroom window, apparently in the hope of trapping him in his room and burning him alive.

Troy raced to the kitchen and got the bucket of drinking water always kept there. Running back, he reached out the window and doused the water on the fire. The fire sputtered, but it didn't go out. He had to get outside and get more water, or the whole house would go up in flames.

Grabbing two buckets, he ran to the front door and leaped outside. A bullet splintered the door jamb by his head, and another thudded into the wall of the house. Like a startled rabbit, he dove back inside.

He was trapped in the burning house, and whoever was out there intended to keep him there.

10.

Troy considered his position. If he stayed inside, he'd be burned to death. If he went outside, he'd be shot.

He spent only a few seconds reaching his decision. Opening the door again, he tossed out the two buckets. No shots came. They were waiting for him. Running to the window, he tried to locate the snipers. There were two, he was sure, from the rapidity of the shots that had been fired when he'd tried to get out. He caught a glimpse of one at the corner of the bunkhouse. He guessed the other one would be at the granary.

With that in mind, he went back to the door. Lifting his six-gun, he checked to make sure it was fully loaded. With the door open, he suddenly dived through, hitting the ground and rolling. Two shots rang out, but neither bullet came close to Troy. He came to one knee and snapped a shot at the bunkhouse corner, then wheeled and fired at the granary.

He doubted if he had hit anything, but he succeeded in silencing both snipers momentarily. Rising to a crouch, he sprinted for the corner of the house. A bullet nicked the house beside his head just as he dived around the corner.

Now he was outside, but still unable to carry water to the fire. He snapped a shot at the bunkhouse, which was closer than the granary. The man at the granary became bolder and fired rapidly, keeping Troy from peeking around to get a shot at him.

Then suddenly more guns entered the melee. Troy risked a look. He saw Willie and Morrie racing down the hill, firing as they came. Apparently they had given up catching the decoys and had been brought back to the ranch by the sound of the gunfire.

The two men hiding by the bunkhouse and granary suddenly broke for their horses and spurred out of the yard, Willie and Morrie in hot pursuit. Troy could see that they had little chance of catching them and he fired once more, this time into the air. It had the desired effect. Morrie and Willie yanked back on their reins, apparently thinking there was still somebody at the buildings shooting at Troy.

When they raced into the yard, Troy met them. "The house is on fire!" he yelled. "I need your help to put it out."

The fire was on the back side of the house, and Willie and Morrie hadn't noticed it yet. Now they threw themselves off their horses and grabbed the buckets Troy had tossed into the yard. While they filled their buckets at the watering trough, Troy got another bucket.

Racing around the corner of the house with his bucket of water, Troy saw that the fire had not gained a great deal of momentum. As a result of the water the three of them splashed on it, the fire soon went out. Some of the wood near the ground was burned, but the house had been saved.

"Reckon we got suckered that time," Willie said disgustedly while they were resting after putting out the fire. "Those fellows we chased out of here had horses that should have been running on race tracks."

"Their job was to get us all away while these other fellows burned the house," Troy said.

"One of us will stick closer to you after this," Morrie promised.

"I don't need a nursemaid," Troy objected. "They're going to get tired of their game after failing as many times as they have."

"You only have to lose once," Willie reminded him.

"Won't make any difference then how many times you've won."

"They're not liable to bother us any more tonight," Troy said. "Let's go to bed."

Troy and Morrie left town in mid afternoon the next day and headed back for the ranch. Just south of town, Troy reined up suddenly, pointing to two riders not far ahead of them, riding slowly along Spring Creek toward the Smoky Hill.

"Looks like Betsy," he said.

Morrie nodded. "And that looks like Rudy Yoeman with her."

"What would they be doing together?" Troy demanded.

"One way to find out," Morrie suggested.

Without a word, both men kicked their horses into a gallop. They were within a hundred yards of the two before they were noticed. The two appeared ready to run, then reined up instead and waited.

"You're picking strange company, Betsy," Troy said through set teeth, pulling up his horse.

"She can choose who she keeps company with," Rudy shot back.

"Reckon she can," Troy agreed. "But it just doesn't seem natural for a house kitten to team up with the wild variety with white stripes down its back."

Yoeman jerked his horse around to face Troy. "Just

who are you calling a polecat?"

Fury surged up in Troy. It was directed as much at Betsy for coming out with Rudy Yoeman as it was at Yoeman himself. But it was Yoeman who offered the chance for him to vent his fury.

"You figure it out," he snapped. "If you want to argue the point, that's fine with me."

"Stop it!" Betsy half screamed. "You're acting like ten-year-old boys. I'm going home."

She reined her horse around toward town, leaving Troy and Yoeman facing each other. Yoeman glared at Troy a moment; then his eyes flicked to Morrie, sitting on his horse only a few feet away.

"There'll be a better time when the odds are even," he snapped, and jerked his horse around and spurred him toward the Smoky Hill.

Troy watched him go, his fury dying slowly. He would bet Yoeman was the kind who never got into a fight willingly unless he had some advantage. He had none here.

Troy suddenly wheeled his horse and went after Betsy, catching her before she was halfway to town. Morrie stayed a discreet distance behind them as he followed them into Peaceful Springs.

"Any explanation as to why you were out riding with Yoeman?" Troy demanded.

"I don't have to account to you for anything," Betsy

101

snapped. "But if it will make you feel better, I heard a woman say in the dress shop today that she heard that someone was planning to do something to the courthouse."

"What are they going to do?" Troy demanded, his anger at Betsy dying.

"That's what I was trying to find out when you butted in," Betsy retorted. "I thought Rudy might know."

"Did he?"

"I didn't get to find out. This woman said she heard that Norge Uldeen had let something slip when he was half drunk."

"Which is all the time," Troy added. "Sorry I flew off the handle, Betsy."

Betsy sighed. "All right. I'll forget it. But you have to trust me a little. I'm on your side, remember."

"I won't forget again," Troy promised.

Betsy reined in behind the dress shop, and Troy rode back toward his own ranch, Morrie falling in with him. Troy told Morrie what Betsy had said.

"Reckon she had a reason for riding with Yoeman," Morrie said. "If Uldeen knows something, it's a good bet that Yoeman knows it, too."

"But Yoeman's not the one to get the information from," Troy said. "Uldeen is the weak link there."

"We'll catch him away from the others one of these

days and see what we can get him to say," Morrie promised.

Troy nodded, but he wasn't satisfied.

"We'll have to find a way to get Norge Uldeen alone and make him talk," he said at the breakfast table the next morning. "We can't wait. If the Mapleton forces are planning to destroy the courthouse, they might do it any time. We've got to find out if there is anything to that rumor."

"We might ride in and keep an eye on the court-house today," Morrie suggested.

"And I'll ride over toward Uldeen's," Willie said. "If he leaves the ranch alone, I'll rope him like a maverick and drag him off where we can talk to him without any interruptions."

"Careful how you manhandle him," Troy warned. "But I think both ideas are good. Let's go. I want to talk to Amos Brush, anyway."

Troy and Morrie rode off to town, while Willie prepared to watch the neighboring ranch. Troy doubted if anything short of a twenty-four-hour-a-day watch on the courthouse would do any good. But at least they should be able to make sure nothing happened to it today.

They had been in town only a short time when Willie came riding in. Troy hadn't even been over to talk to the lawyer.

"Just saw Norge Uldeen heading for town," Willie reported to Troy. "Thought we might get him cornered somewhere in town and ask him some questions."

"Nothing loosens his tongue like whiskey," Morrie said.

"You get the whiskey," Willie said. "I'll find out where he goes."

Troy went over to talk to Brush, while Willie and Morrie prepared for Uldeen's visit to town. Brush had found more character witnesses, but admitted they needed more than that. After half an hour, Troy left the lawyer's office and went down the street. He finally found Morrie and Willie coming out of the hardware store.

"What did you find out?" he asked.

"Nothing yet," Morrie said. "We gave Norge the bottle, and he drank it down like it was water. Passed out before he said anything worth-while."

"But we put the fear in him before he passed out," Willie said with a big grin. "We said he was going to kill himself drinking like that. And he'd sure go to hell if he died without telling the truth about everything."

"He was drunk enough to believe Willie, too," Morrie added.

"Where is he now?" Troy asked.

"Come here and let us show you," Willie said.

Willie led the way through the hardware store to the back where the storekeeper kept some coffins. In one, with the lid off, was Norge Uldeen, laid out as if he were dead. His hands were folded across his chest, and a candle was burning at either end of the coffin.

"When he wakes up and sees where he is—" Willie said in anticipation.

Troy couldn't help grinning. "He'll either tell everything he knows or kill himself getting out of there."

"We're going to be right here to see which it is," Willie promised.

11.

Norge Uldeen seldom stayed unconscious long when he drank himself into a stupor. This time was no exception. Troy and Morrie took turns moving around the store while they waited. But Willie didn't leave the coffin in the back of the hardware store.

Shortly after noon, Uldeen stirred a little. Troy stepped to the door and called Morrie, who was in front of the hardware.

All three were there, as well as the store owner, when Uldeen pried one eye open and tried to look around. He obviously couldn't get things in focus. After a couple of minutes he tried again, and this time he saw the candle at the foot of the coffin. He tried to sit up but with little success.

"Where am I?" he demanded thickly.

"Dead," Willie said in a solemn tone, "You drank

yourself to death. Now you'll have to pay for your sins."

The blur came out of Uldeen's eyes, and he hunched himself up on his elbows. His neck turned like an owl's, and he saw the candle at the head of the coffin. Then his eyes fell on the coffin itself, and he realized where he was.

His scream was something between the wail of a banshee and the dying cry of a panther. With a leap that Troy wouldn't have believed possible, he came out of the coffin and hit the floor, running with all the speed his wobbly legs could muster.

He was through the partition door and halfway down the aisle of the hardware store before those watching could comprehend what was happening and go after him. Willie, who could run faster than either Morrie or Troy, caught Uldeen half a block up the street and lifted him off the walk. But Uldeen's feet kept churning as though he were trying to break the world speed record.

"Where are you going?" Willie demanded.

"Got to find the preacher," Uldeen babbled. "Got to find the preacher."

"Want to tell the truth about some things?" Willie insisted.

"I'll confess," Uldeen said, his eyes fairly popping out of his head. "I'll confess."

"The preacher's out of town," Willie said. "You tell

me, and I'll see that he hears it."

Uldeen squirmed in Willie's grasp, his voice bordering on hysteria. "I've got to find him. I can't die without telling him."

"Telling him what?" Willie demanded, shaking the little man.

"That I know they're going to blow up the courthouse."

Troy and Morrie were with Willie by now. They stared at each other, then at Norge Uldeen. Uldeen was still so frightened he could barely speak intelligibly.

"Who's going to do it?" Willie demanded.

"They're going to," Uldeen said. "They're going to."

It was obvious that Uldeen wasn't going to make any more sense than that.

Finally Willie took a bottle from his pocket and handed it to Uldeen. "This will settle you down," he said.

Uldeen looked as if he were afraid of the bottle. But habit forced him to grab it and take a big swallow. It seemed to drive away his hysteria, and he glared around at the three men near him, then hunched over and scooted down the street toward his horse.

"Let's find out if he's telling the truth," Troy suggested.

"Just how are we going to do that?" Morrie demanded. "Are you going to go around and ask who 'they' are and if they're going to blow up the courthouse?"

"About the only thing anyone could use to blow up a building the size of the courthouse would be dynamite," Troy explained. "And the only place where there is any dynamite around here is that little shed behind the courthouse where they stored the dynamite they used in building the bridge south of town. Let's find out if any has been stolen."

Morrie and Willie quickly agreed to that. Troy found the sheriff, who had a key to the building, went back to the shed, and the sheriff unlocked the door. Sheriff Hanson also had an inventory of the amount of dynamite stored in the shed. When he checked that list against the dynamite found there, his eyes widened.

"A full case of dynamite is gone," he said. "That would be enough to blow half of Peaceful Springs off the map."

"Small town," Troy muttered.

But the sheriff's implication was plain. Somebody had stolen enough dynamite from the shed to damage the courthouse beyond repair. Then it wouldn't be hard to convince undecided voters to mark their ballots in favor of building the new courthouse in

Mapleton rather than in little Peaceful Springs. But as long as the courthouse was there and in good shape, voters with an eye on keeping their taxes down might cast their votes to use what they already had instead of spending so much money to build a new courthouse in Mapleton.

"I'll put a guard around the courthouse night and day," the sheriff said, more to himself than to those near him. "If they want to move everything to Mapleton, that's fine with me. But they're not going to pull a dirty trick like this to get the job done."

Word quickly spread through town about the missing dynamite and what Uldeen had said about blowing up the courthouse. Indignation soared. Within three hours, the sheriff had the men of the town organized into shifts to stand guard around the courthouse. Morrie signed up to take a turn, but he and Willie convinced the sheriff not to put Troy on the list. Considering the lengths to which the Detts had already gone to kill Troy, it would be foolish to put him on guard duty where he would be exposed to an easy attack by a killer.

Before leaving town, Troy stopped at the dress shop. Vivian looked weary and worried.

"Some people think I'm a spy," she said. "They can't forget that I came from Mapleton. And they won't believe that I'm fighting as hard as they are to keep the county seat here. My business will go to pot, too, if Mapleton wins."

"The sheriff's going to guard the courthouse now," Troy said. He looked into the rear of the shop. "I see Betsy is back at work."

Vivian shrugged. "If you want to talk to her, go ahead. We're not that busy."

Troy shook his head. "She was out riding with Rudy Yoeman yesterday," he said. "That surprised me."

"She was after information, she told me. Here's something else that may surprise you, too. She insists she was with Rafe Dett when your father was killed. I believe her, Troy."

Troy shook his head. "She told me she saw him in Tower; she didn't say she was with him. But who else would kill Pa?"

"I don't know," Vivian said. "But Betsy says she was with Rafe, and I think she was. If that's so, he didn't kill your father."

Troy didn't argue with Vivian, but as soon as he left the dress shop, he headed for the hotel. Al Theim should know whether Betsy had been with Rafe Dett that day or not.

Al Theim shied away from Troy's direct question like a gun shy horse at the sound of a cannon.

"I can't keep track of a girl like Betsy all the time," he snapped. "I know she wasn't home that afternoon.

But I can't believe she was at Tower. I'd skin her alive if I found out she was with a varmint like Rafe."

"Does she always tell you everything she does?" Troy asked.

"That's a dirty question to ask about the girl you intend to marry," Theim snapped. Then he sighed heavily. "But I guess you've got a right to ask. She does lie to me once in a while. I think all youngsters lie to their parents sometimes."

Troy frowned. He doubted that. But he didn't doubt that Betsy had lied to her father.

Morrie took his turn guarding the courthouse. The sheriff kept four men on duty during the night hours and at least two men near the courthouse during the day. But when Morrie was gone, Troy found that Willie was his constant shadow.

Troy divided his time between trying to find evidence for his defense against the murder charge and helping in the drive for votes for Peaceful Springs in the approaching election. He didn't spend much time working on the ranch, although there was plenty to be done.

There was no attempt made to damage the courthouse. Troy was sure that the guard the sheriff had posted was foiling the planned attempt to blow up the building. Sheriff Hanson promised to keep the guard there until after the election.

The trial date for Troy was approaching with alarming speed, too. It wouldn't be until some time after the election, but considering the lack of a solid defense, it was coming entirely too fast.

Then Willie found a note pinned on the bunkhouse door one evening when he and Troy came home from town. Morrie was to be on night guard duty at the courthouse, so he had stayed in town. The note was addressed to Troy, and Willie brought it to him without opening it.

Troy opened the note and read it quickly. It was printed crudely on an old scrap of paper.

"What does it say?" Willie demanded.

Troy handed him the note. "Just to keep out of the election campaign," he said. "That doesn't make any sense. I'm not doing the Mapleton forces any more damage than dozens of others over here. Maybe they all got notes like this."

Willie shook his head. "I doubt it. Looks to me like somebody is working up an excuse to come gunning for you. It ain't the election that's bothering this fellow."

"Well, it's nothing to lose sleep over," Troy said. "We've got to get ready for that rally over at Elkhorn tomorrow. Morrie will probably be too tired to go, after standing guard tonight."

"It's going to be touch and go with some of those

people over there," Willie predicted. "This election doesn't mean much to them. But their votes will count as much as yours or mine."

Morrie had just come home the next morning when another rider charged into the yard. Troy took one look at him and rushed out of the house. Al Theim didn't ride a horse often, and Troy had never seen him ride one like this.

Theim yanked back on the reins, sliding his horse to a stop. Troy and Morrie and Willie clustered around him.

"What's wrong, Al?" Troy demanded.

"It's Betsy," Theim said. "She's gone. Didn't come home at all last night."

Troy stared at Al Theim. "Did she say where she was going?"

"She just went for a ride like she does almost every decent day," Theim said. "But she didn't come back. Something has happened to her."

"We'll find her," Troy said. "Willie, you and I will go look for her. Morrie, you get some sleep."

"What about our trip to Elkhorn today?" Willie asked.

"Maybe you'd better go with Mary and Doris," Troy said. "I'll look for Betsy."

Willie shook his head. "I'll look, too. They can get along without me."

114

Troy didn't argue. He ran to the corral and saddled his horse.

"Where to first?" Willie asked when he had his own horse saddled.

"Town," Troy said. "We've got to tell Doris and Mary we're not going with them to Elkhorn. And I want to talk to Vivian."

It had suddenly struck Troy that Betsy might have told Vivian that she had explained to her parents that she was spending the night with her so Vivian wouldn't say anything. That would be one way of hitting back at Al Theim if Betsy had had a bad argument with him. Betsy had been particularly nice to Troy lately, but he wasn't at all sure she had been that nice to her parents.

In town, Troy rode to Vivian's first. If Betsy was there, he and Willie wouldn't have to cancel their trip to Elkhorn. But Vivian hadn't seen Betsy since noon the day before, when she had said she wanted to take a long ride out in the country. Vivian had been worried when she hadn't come back to work, and now she became almost frantic when she learned that she hadn't gone home, either.

Troy rode around and told Mary, but insisted that Mary and Doris go on to Elkhorn. There was little the two could do that the men of the town couldn't do.

"Now what?" Willie asked.

115

"Uldeen's place," Troy said without hesitation.

Willie nodded. "You figure the Detts or some of their kin must be involved in anything aimed at you. Maybe you're right, too. The Detts are after you, and they'd know they could hit you hardest by grabbing your girl."

It took only a few minutes for Troy and Willie to ride to the Dett ranch, where Norge Uldeen was nominally in charge. Troy eyed all the buildings as he approached, looking for Rudy. If Betsy was being held there, it could very easily be a trap to ambush him. But he didn't see anything suspicious. Norge and Hilda Uldeen came out on the porch when he and Willie came into the yard. Libby Dett appeared behind them.

"Betsy Theim is missing," Troy announced. "We wondered if any of you had seen her."

"Why would she come here?" Libby demanded, stepping around the Uldeens and down the porch steps to the yard. "Do you think we kidnapped her?"

"I was just asking if you'd seen her," Troy said testily.

"Well, we haven't," Libby snapped back. "I'll saddle up and help you look, if that will make you feel better."

"The only thing that's going to make me feel better is to find out where she is," Troy shot back. "She didn't come home at all last night."

"Maybe she's a wild one," Hilda Uldeen said.

"Not that wild," Troy snapped angrily.

"Well, she ain't here," Hilda said. "I ain't one to have any hand in kidnapping."

"None of us are," Libby said furiously. "You've got your nerve coming here looking for Betsy."

"I intend to look everywhere till I find her," Troy said.

Wheeling his horse, he kicked him into a run out of the yard. Willie followed without a word. Troy tried to decide where to look next. He knew that Betsy often rode down the Smoky Hill River. Maybe she had done that yesterday and somehow had been thrown and hurt.

His ranch was near the river, and as he was passing close to the corrals, he saw Morrie waving at him. Troy reined into the yard, Willie following.

"Thought you'd be asleep," Troy said. "What's wrong?"

"Heard somebody galloping out of the yard a few minutes ago," Morrie said. "Woke me up. I found this note on the door. It's for you." He handed a paper to Troy.

Troy read it and felt as if a mule had kicked him.

12.

As Troy stared at the note, Willie edged his horse closer. "You look like you just swallowed a frog," he said. "What does it say?"

"We've got Betsy," Troy read. "If you want her back, stop pushing Peaceful Springs in the election."

"Who is we?" Willie demanded.

"You didn't expect them to sign it, did you?" Morrie grunted.

"That's sure a mighty thin excuse for kidnapping anybody," Troy said. "They could have done a lot of things simpler than that to keep me from working for Peaceful Springs."

"There's got to be more to it than that," Morrie agreed. "Did you see that PS at the bottom?"

Troy's eyes shot back to the paper in his hand. He had been so stunned by the note that he had failed to notice the smaller printing at the bottom of the paper.

"There will be a letter at the hotel for John Garfunkle. That's you."

"That letter may give the real reason they've kidnapped Betsy," Morrie said.

Troy nodded. "Let's go."

"I'll stay here," Morrie said. "Could be this is just another trick to get us all away from the ranch so they can burn it."

Troy nodded, but he was already wheeling his horse toward town, Willie following. Their horses were puffing hard from the run when they reined up in front of the hotel. Al Theim had seen them racing up the street and was on the wide porch of the hotel when they stopped.

"Have you heard anything about Betsy?" he demanded.

Troy nodded as he swung from the saddle. "Have you got a letter here for a John Garfunkle?"

"I just brought it up from the post office when I came back from your ranch," Al Theim said. "Where's Betsy?"

"I'm John Garfunkle, and I'm supposed to get that letter," Troy said. "It may tell us where Betsy is."

Al turned into the hotel with Troy and Willie. "I figured somebody by that name would be coming to spend the night at the hotel, and this letter was to catch him here." Theim took the letter from a pigeonhole behind the desk.

Troy handed Al the note he had gotten out at his ranch, then snatched the letter from Theim's hand and ripped it open. Al Theim sank into a chair as Troy read the note. Troy ignored him and pulled the letter from the envelope. It was printed just like the note he'd gotten at the ranch.

"If you want Betsy back, come after her yourself. And come alone. We'll kill her if you try any tricks. Come down the Smoky. You'll know it when you get here."

Al Theim came up out of his chair, waving the paper in his hand frantically. "We've got to get her back right now!" he shouted.

Emma Theim came from the kitchen, wiping her hands on her apron. "What is going on out here?" she demanded. "Have you heard from Betsy?"

Al waved the paper at his wife. "She's been kidnapped. We're going after her."

"Hold on," Troy shouted. "Read this before you go off half cocked. I've got to go after her alone."

"Why?" Theim demanded, grabbing the paper from Troy's hands. After running his eyes over it, he looked up. "Why do they want you to come after her? Why not me?"

"They want to kill him," Willie said. "That's why they're asking him to come alone."

"You'll have to go," Al Theim said. "We can't take a chance that they might kill Betsy."

Troy looked at Theim, so scared he was drooling. He reminded Troy of a whipped dog. "I'm going," he said. "Alone. We don't know who has Betsy or why they took her. Until we know that, we can't afford to take any chances."

"If you don't bring her back, I'll go out and kill every one of them!" Al Theim sputtered, rubbing a sleeve across his chin to wipe off the spit.

"I'll go with you, Troy," Willie said quietly.

Troy shook his head. "They said to come alone. That's how I'm going."

Emma came out to Troy's horse as he mounted. "If there is anything we can do, let us know. We'll do anything."

"Just stay home and keep out of it," Troy said. "And don't worry any more than you have to."

Troy wheeled his horse and galloped down the street toward the road leading to his ranch, Willie beside him.

"Emma will hold up," Willie said. "But I don't know what Al's going to do."

Troy nodded. "He's too scared right now to do anything. But when he has time to think about it, he's liable to go off half cocked and get himself and maybe some of the rest of us killed."

"How about me and Morrie following you if we keep back out of sight?" Willie asked.

Troy shook his head. "The note says to come alone. They may have somebody watching to make sure nobody follows me."

"The only reason for them to demand that you come alone is so they can get you away from us where they can kill you," Willie said.

"That's possible," Troy admitted. "But if they're that set on getting at me, they very likely would kill Betsy just from pure cussedness. I'll be mighty careful."

Willie sighed. "I hope being careful is enough."

Troy quickly explained to Morrie about the letter to John Garfunkle then went into the house and gathered up enough food to last him for a couple of meals.

"Must think they're a long way down the creek," Morrie said.

"Just a precaution," Troy said. He pocketed an extra handful of ammunition for his revolver and checked to make sure his rifle was fully loaded. "I expect to be back by dark, but don't worry if I'm not."

"Reckon we'll worry till you're back, if it's only an hour from now." Morrie said.

Troy hurried out to his horse, jammed the rifle into its boot and swung up. "Remember, the note said I was to come alone," he warned, glaring at his two hired hands.

He kicked his horse into a gallop down the river bank. And it wasn't easy to kill a man, even from ambush, when someone was with him.

He didn't doubt, however, that Betsy would be in real danger if the kidnappers saw someone with Troy when he came after her. Alone, he was like a dead man riding to his own funeral, but Betsy should be safe.

The sun passed its zenith, and still Troy rode down the river, approaching with extreme caution any place where an ambush could be laid. He didn't expect to surprise the kidnappers. He just hoped somehow to keep them from surprising him.

He stopped some time after noon and ate some of the food he had brought along. Then he put the rest back in the saddlebag and nudged his horse into a trot again. He estimated he was twelve or thirteen miles from his ranch now and near the big bend in the river where it swung back to the southwest for a way. He recalled a dugout down in the loop where the river turned back again on its easterly course. Some fellow had homesteaded that place and given up on it, leaving the dugout with the sod roof abandoned. That would be a good place to hide out to avoid accidental detection. The road running along the northern bank of the river cut across the loop, not going near the dugout, hitting the river again farther to the east.

Troy reined up, wondering if he should investigate. At that moment, Ike Dett rose up from a shallow gully beside the road just ahead of him.

Don't reach for your gun, Prescott!" he snapped. "It will be the last move you'll ever make."

Troy carefully held his hands on the saddle horn as he faced Ike Dett standing in the gully, his gun trained on Troy. Troy considered his chances of diving sideways and trying for his gun as he fell. But then another voice cut in from behind him. Troy's head snapped around. Rudy Yoeman was there, some distance from the road, standing in another gully.

They had selected their ambush carefully. The prairie was smooth enough there so that Troy hadn't suspected a trap.

While Ike stepped up to where he could hold his gun directly on Troy, Rudy took Troy's gun from its holster and jerked the rifle out of its boot. Troy was surprised that he was still alive. Surely this had all been staged just to kill him. But maybe not right here. Ike ordered Troy to dismount and made him walk ahead of him away from the road, down into the loop of the river toward the abandoned dugout. Yoeman led Troy's horse.

"You sure nobody came with you?" Ike demanded.

"You can see for yourself," Troy said.

"We can't see who's two miles behind you."

"That letter said to come alone."

124

"I know what it said," Ike said worriedly. "I just don't know what you did about it."

They reached the dugout, and Ike called a halt. "I'll take him inside," he told Yoeman. "You ride back a few miles and make sure nobody is following him. If there is, don't do nothing about it. Just get back here as quick as you can. We'll kill Prescott and leave him here for them to find. We'll let them know we mean what we say."

Yoeman started to protest but stopped when he met Ike Dett's stare. He got his horse from the corral and galloped off to follow the river back toward Peaceful Springs. Troy watched him leave, hoping that Morrie and Willie had stayed at the ranch as he had told them to.

Ike jabbed the gun in Troy's back and pushed him through the upper door and down the steps into the dugout. When he stumbled through the inner door, he saw Betsy sitting dejectedly on the bed. Troy was pushed into a chair across the room.

"Are you all right, Betsy?" Troy asked.

Betsy nodded. "They haven't hurt me. It was you they were after."

"I figured that," Troy said, wondering if he would be killed now.

Ike dropped down on a stool near the door, his gun still on Troy.

It was growing dark inside the dugout when Rudy Yoeman returned. The October chill was creeping into the room, and Ike, after hearing his report that no one was following Troy, immediately ordered him outside to bring in an armload of cow chips to start the fire.

Once the fire was started, Ike ordered Rudy to get a sack lying in the corner and hang it over the one small window above ground level. Then he lit a candle that he produced from his pocket.

"You think of everything, don't you?" Betsy asked, frowning at Ike.

"A lot more than you figure," Ike said, obviously pleased with the way things were going. He turned to Troy. "Now that we know there is no one following you, we can get down to business. When we finish, you and Betsy can go home. Fair enough?"

Troy eyed Ike suspiciously. "We don't have any business," he said.

"Watch him, Rudy," Ike said. While Rudy got his gun in his hand, Ike moved over to stand in front of Troy. "We've got business all right, and the sooner we get it over with, the better it is going to be for everyone."

Ike cuffed Troy's ear with an open palm, making his head ring.

"Now I'm not going to waste time on you, Prescott," he said. "I'd kill you in a minute if I didn't want something worse than to see you dead. That's that ranch of yours. It cuts our land right in two. You sign it over without causing any trouble, and you can ride out of here scot-free. Now in your situation, you can't ask for anything better than that."

"Once I sign over my place, you'll kill me, anyway," Troy said.

"I'll do it before you sign if you get too smart," Ike said, scowling.

He dug a piece of paper out of his pocket and laid it on the table. "Move your chair up there and read that. It's all legal. You sell me that ranch of yours for ten dollars an acre."

Troy frowned and looked at the paper. Ten dollars an acre was a fair price. The document was legal, as he had expected it to be. Deek Dett, Ike's brother, was a lawyer, and he apparently had drawn up the deed.

"Let's see the ten dollars an acre," Troy said.

"That's what I'm charging you for your freedom," Ike said. "Keeping alive is surely worth that much to you."

"What about Betsy?"

Ike shrugged. "She can go home with you just as soon as you sign that."

Troy considered.

"I won't do it," he said.

Ike grabbed Troy's arm and jerked him off the chair, then kicked the chair halfway across the room.

His fist came around and caught Troy on the side of the jaw. Troy lost his balance and fell, skidding almost to the bed. Betsy didn't move, and Troy was glad of it. Ike wouldn't be loath to beat her up, too.

"Get back on that chair," Ike ordered. "Sit there till you're ready to sign."

"I'm not signing anything," Troy said, getting to his feet.

"Tie him to the chair," Ike ordered Rudy, and went back to his stool, his gun still trained on Troy. "We've got lots of time. He'll change his mind before morning." The threat was unmistakable.

Rudy picked up some rope that had been lying in the corner, apparently for just this purpose, and wrapped it around Troy and the chair. Then he threw more chips on the fire, swearing because the chimney wasn't drawing right and some of the acrid smoke was sifting into the room.

Troy watched Ike carefully, expecting him to come over and start beating him again. Or maybe he would begin on Betsy, figuring correctly that that would soften up Troy's resistance more quickly.

Suddenly Ike came to his feet, his gun turned on the door. Troy listened and heard the sound of a horse out in the yard. Then the outside door squealed as it opened. Ike squared away, facing the inner door. When it opened, whoever came in would be dead the instant he showed himself.

But the inner door didn't burst open. A knock sounded instead. Ike eased to one side of the door. "Who is it?" he demanded.

"Libby," the voice said. Then the door swung inward. She glared at Ike with the gun. "I figured you'd shoot me if I didn't tell you who was coming in."

"How did you know we were here?" Ike demanded.

"I made Norge tell me," Libby said.

Ike wheeled on Rudy Yoeman. "You blabbermouth! I ought to kill you. Who else beside Norge did you tell about this?"

"Nobody," Rudy said, scowling. "He followed me around like a bucket calf and I had to tell him to keep him from riding into town and stirring up everybody with some wild stories. Anyhow, he's in favor of what we're doing."

"The fewer people who know about it, the better off we are," Ike said.

"Now you listen to me," Libby said sternly, pushing up to within a few inches of Ike. "We all agreed, including Pa, that we'd let the law take care of Troy."

"The law ain't going to do nothing, and you know it," Ike growled. "Besides, having him hung for shooting Rafe ain't going to get that land we need. This way we get it all done at one time."

If Troy had had any doubts about Ike's intentions once Troy signed over his land, they were gone now.

129

13.

Troy braced himself as Ike moved toward him, swinging an open palm against the side of Troy's head.

"I'm going to give you just two minutes to sign that paper," he yelled. "If you don't, I'm going to kill you inch by inch."

Libby jerked her attention away from Rudy and Betsy. "You just pull in your horns, big brother!" she snapped. "We'll do it Pa's way."

"Pa ain't going to cry if he's dead," Ike said.

"You used Betsy just for bait, didn't you?" Libby accused. "Like little kids playing games."

"We got him. That's what counts." Ike turned his eyes on his sister. "You want that land, too. Don't forget that."

"I don't steal what I want," Libby said. She turned

and glared at Rudy. "I wouldn't be surprised if it was Rudy's idea to kidnap Betsy."

Rudy came to his feet. "Now just what do you mean by that?"

"You seem to be enjoying your captive a great deal," Libby said sharply.

"Now hold on, Libby," Rudy protested. "We're just trying to get that land for our ranch."

Libby wheeled away from Rudy as Ike slammed a fist into Troy's face.

"Now you sign that paper quick, Prescott, or you'll wish you were dead!" Ike yelled.

"You'll kill me, anyway," Troy said, "but you're not going to have a legal title to that land."

Ike hit Troy again, putting all his two hundred and forty pounds behind the blow. Troy managed to jerk his head back so that Ike's fist only grazed his chin. But still his senses reeled and lights flashed in front of his eyes.

Libby charged at Ike, slapping his face. It reminded Troy of a terrier going after a mastiff. But Ike didn't strike back at his sister.

"You listen to me, Ike," Libby shouted. "You claim you're no coward. But if you kill Troy while he's tied up, I'm going to tell the whole country that you're the biggest coward that ever walked."

"Shut up!" Ike screamed. But he didn't hit Troy

again. Troy's brain was clearing fast. He was amazed at the power Libby seemed to hold over her huge brother. Libby was defending him, Troy knew, not because she wanted to keep him alive but to keep Ike from committing a cold-blooded murder.

Ike still stood in front of Troy, glaring at him. But Libby grabbed the other chair and put it beside Troy's and sat down beside him, facing Ike. Ike growled like a wounded bear, but he backed off to the stool by the door and sat down. For the moment, Libby had stopped Ike from killing Troy. But the stalemate couldn't last.

Betsy turned to Rudy Yoeman with an inviting look, and he didn't turn down the invitation. When he moved closer to her, she snuggled up next to him and apparently shut out everything else in the room. Rudy obviously didn't object.

But Libby did. She left her chair and charged at the two. Troy expected her to tear Rudy away from Betsy. But she grabbed Betsy by the hair instead. In a moment, a free-swinging, hair-pulling brawl erupted between the two girls. With an oath that shook the sod roof of the dugout, Ike charged across the room, grabbed one girl with either hand and tore them apart as a boy would separate two fighting bugs.

"Worse than two little school kids," Ike shouted. He slammed Betsy back on the bed and shoved Libby halfway across the room.

Troy was surprised at the ease with which he handled the two. His strength matched his size. Betsy was livid with rage, and when Libby came back to sit beside Troy again, she erupted.

"Let her have him if she wants him," she shouted at Rudy and Ike. "You don't have to get Troy to sign anything to get that land. His pa mortgaged that ranch to the hilt. If he doesn't pay it off, it will go to the bank. Then you can buy it cheap without dealing with Troy."

Ike's face lit up like a rising sun. Troy knew what this meant, although he doubted if Betsy did.

But Libby did. Her fists clenched, and when Ike came off his stool toward them, she hurled herself at him. This time she didn't say a word but just blocked his path.

"Get out of my way!" Ike roared, pushing against her.

Libby held her ground, shoving against his great strength. Troy tried desperately to get the ropes off his arms, but he couldn't manage it. He saw Rudy come off the bed in response to Ike's shout to get Libby out of his way. Betsy, her face registering shock at what she had started, came to her feet. But it was too late to change things now.

Troy tipped his chair backward to escape Ike's rush

smoke was going to kill him as surely as Ike would have.

Then suddenly someone burst into the room. Troy's eyes were watering so much he couldn't see who it was. His first thought was that it must be Ike, coming back to make sure Troy was dead.

Then the man stumbled over Troy's chair, and Troy grunted. The man dropped on his knees, and Troy recognized Morrie. Morrie's hands flew as he took a knife from his belt and cut the ropes.

"How did you get here?" Troy choked.

"Willie and me followed you. Hid out when that fellow came riding our way, then followed him here." Morrie coughed. "Let's get out of here."

Morrie was coughing violently now as he led Troy to the stairway, where some fresh air was coming in.

"Where's Willie?"

"Outside," Morrie said, breathing deeply of the fresh air, "making sure those jaspers don't start shooting at us when we come out."

Troy suddenly remembered Libby and jerked away from Morrie. In spite of Morrie's protests, he dived back into the smoke-filled room. Holding his breath, he plunged toward the spot where he had seen Libby fall. He heard her coughing but still almost stepped on her before he saw her. Stooping, he picked her up and groped for the door; Morrie led the way up the stairs.

Troy looked around for Ike and Rudy, but there

as Ike, not waiting for Rudy's assistance, slammed Libby aside with a blow that Troy knew must have knocked her unconscious if it hadn't killed her. He tried to escape Ike and struggle toward Libby as acrid smoke suddenly filled the room. At the first breath of it, Troy choked. He saw the yellow smoke billowing out of the stove. He'd never known cow chips to give off smoke like that.

Ike was almost on top of him when he suddenly began choking and staggered back, trying to sweep away the smoke with his hand. The stove was smoking violently now with a putrid smoke that was choking everyone.

Ike suddenly forgot his lethal intentions and staggered toward the door, groping blindly for the latch. Through the smoke which was blinding Troy, too, Troy saw Rudy and Betsy following Ike to the door.

The door jerked open and the three, coughing and gasping, pushed each other in their effort to get up the steps to the outer door. Troy heard that door open, too; then the coughing faded.

Troy recognized the smell of sulphur, but he couldn't think how sulphur could have gotten in the stove. He tried to jerk the chair closer to the door in the hope that some fresh air might filter down from outside. But all his efforts went into coughing. The

135

wasn't enough light, and his eyes were still watering so he couldn't see much. Willie whispered to them from near the outside door.

"They went to their horses," he said. "Let's get out while the getting is good."

Troy followed Willie and Morrie back up the slope where they had left their horses. Suddenly a shot ripped the air, coming from the spot where Ike and Rudy had tied their horses.

"Spread out," Morrie whispered, and shoved a gun into Troy's hand. "Now all of us start shooting at once."

Willie fired the first shot from off to Troy's right. Troy fired immediately, and so did Morrie to his left. He heard a shout from Rudy down below.

"The whole town must have come out after her! Let's get out of here!"

There was no more shooting. Horses pounded down to the river and splashed across. Troy turned his attention to Libby, the first chance he'd had to see if she was all right. She was still coughing, an involuntary reaction to the smoke she had inhaled. Gently he lifted her head and put it on his knee.

"Where did you get that sulphur?" Troy asked.

"In town," Morrie said. "We guessed they might hole up in some shack if they didn't kill you outright. Willie thought of bringing the sulphur to smoke them out."

Within a few minutes, Libby started to revive.

"You're going to be all right," Troy said. "That smoke almost got you."

"Ike hit me," Libby whispered incredulously, coughing again. "How did you get me out here?"

"Long story," Troy said.

"We'll check to see if they left any horses," Morrie said. "We'll be right back."

Morrie and Willie disappeared in the dark, and Troy helped Libby sit up, then told her what had happened while she was unconscious.

"Why did you go back after me?" she asked when he finished, "I'd think you'd want to get as far away as possible from every Dett."

"From some of them, maybe," Troy admitted, "but not you. You stood up for me, remember? That's why Ike slugged you. I was just returning the favor."

She nodded. "I owe you some thanks."

"Not half as much as I owe you," he said. "Besides, you're something special."

She looked at him like a startled bird. He could see the surprise on her face even in the dim light. "I hope you don't mean a special enemy," she said finally.

"I don't," he said.

She was quiet then till Morrie and Willie came back, leading two horses.

"Guess they were so excited they took only the

horses they could ride. Betsy must have gone with them."

"They probably made her go," Troy said. "But I don't think they'll hurt her. They won't drag us into any more ambushes trying to rescue her, that's sure."

"They kidnapped her just to get their hands on you," Libby said. "Let's get away from this place."

Willie ran back to the dugout and jumped up on the roof, taking a flat tin off the top of the stovepipe that protruded from the roof.

"Guess we don't have any more skunks to smoke out of there," he said, and sailed the tin away.

In spite of Morrie's warnings that they should stay as far away from the Dett ranch as possible, Troy insisted on riding past there to see that Libby got home safely. Then the three men rode on to Troy's ranch. It was well after midnight when they got there, but Troy was too tired to care. Willie still insisted that he was going to stand guard till morning.

It was after noon when Troy rode into town the next day. Since it was Sunday, he found both Mary and Doris at home. They reported on their meeting in Elkhorn.

"They're divided down there," Mary said. "They're almost as close to Mapleton as they are to Peaceful Springs, and somebody from Mapleton has been down there promising them bonuses if they vote to move the county seat."

"But there are three big families that they didn't get to," Doris added. "We promised them we'd get them to the polls if they'd vote our way. I think they will."

"If they could come to Elkhorn for the meeting, why can't they come to vote?" Troy asked.

"Only one man came to the meeting. There are about half a dozen voters out there, some of them crippled or too old to make the trip in a lumber wagon. We promised them a ride in a buggy. If we don't do it, somebody from Mapleton might. Then Mapleton will get their votes."

Troy nodded. "We'll need about two buggies."

"I'll round up the buggies and teams," Mary said. "I could even drive one."

"Willie and me can drive them," Morrie said.

"The election is next Tuesday," Mary reminded him.

Troy explained what had happened the day before, but he made light of the danger he had been in.

It began raining Monday night, and election day dawned cold and dismal, with rain coming down steadily. Troy stared out the window, thinking that this was going to be a miserable day to drive all the way to Elkhorn and take voters to the polls.

But when he got to town, along with Willie and Morrie, he discovered that Mary and Doris were in high spirits.

"This rain could keep a lot of people home," Mary

said. "Mapleton has to get sixty percent of the eligible voters to vote yes to win. Everybody who stays home counts as a no vote."

Troy grinned. "This kind of weather ought to keep everybody home but a duck."

As soon as the polls opened, Troy cast his own vote, then headed down the Smoky Hill River with Morrie and Willie. Willie knew how to find the three Negro families who needed transportation to the polls.

"Sure seems like a long way to go to get just a few votes," Morrie grumbled as he sat beside Troy. Willie was driving the other buggy.

"Would be, except everybody thinks this is going to be very close," Troy said. "Just a half-dozen votes may decide it."

They found the families shortly after noon and loaded them in the buggies with the tops to shield them from the rain. They seemed glad enough to get to ride to the polls in some comfort.

But two miles from Elkhorn, Troy, who was driving in the lead, was suddenly stopped by two men who rode over a knoll directly into the path of his buggy. He reined in sharply when he saw that one of the men was holding a gun.

Twisting his head toward the buggy Willie was driving, he discovered that he was also being held up by armed men. Neither Troy nor Morrie had a chance to reach for his gun.

14.

"We're taking your passengers," one of the men said. They had their hats pulled low over their faces against the rain, and Troy couldn't recognize any of them. Probably they were strangers to him, anyway. Jake Dett had a lot of men working for him whom Troy had never seen.

Troy looked back and saw that Willie had had no chance to resist, either.

Just then a big coach came over the hill. These were the voters Doris had said the Mapleton boosters hadn't reached. She was so sure they would vote for whoever did the most for them that she had promised them a way of getting to the polls to assure their votes for Peaceful Springs. Apparently the Mapleton forces had reached the same conclusion. And now Mapleton was going to take them to the polls in high style. And

141

it would be a much more comfortable ride in an enclosed coach than in buggies. These votes, a half-dozen of them, would go for Mapleton now.

The people in the buggies eagerly climbed out and into the big coach, squeezing in when it got crowded. But it was dry there. They barely looked back at the buggies they had been riding in.

"That is the sneakiest thing I ever saw!" Morrie exploded. "I wouldn't be half as mad if they'd taken my money."

"I know what you mean," Troy said, fighting his own anger. "If they were so determined to take them to the polls to get their votes, why didn't they come out this morning and take them all the way?"

"Made us make the long trip and waste the whole day and then lose," Morrie said. "If I ever see that guy who pulled his gun on us, I'll kill him like I would a bug?"

"Let's go home," Troy said. "We're not going to do ourselves or anybody else any good down here now."

It was almost dark when they got back to Peaceful Springs. Mary and Doris were furious when Troy related what had happened.

"I've heard of some strange hold-ups," Mary said. "But I never heard of anyone stealing voters."

"People here have turned out like it was a sunny day," Doris said. "I'll bet they did over in Mapleton, too. If they were desperate enough to pull a stunt like stealing those voters, they sure wouldn't let their own voters in Mapleton stay home."

"Put the teams and buggies away," Mary suggested; "then come back to the courthouse, and we'll watch the votes add up as each township sends in its report."

Willie rode out to check on the ranch, while Troy and Morrie went to the courthouse. When Willie didn't come back to town within an hour, Troy relaxed. Apparently nothing had happened to the ranch while they were gone.

The first townships to report were the ones close to Peaceful Springs. Peaceful Springs Township itself had voted almost unanimously to keep the county seat where it was. Troy guessed that those on the Dett ranch were probably responsible for the few Yes votes that had been registered.

Western Township, just to the west of Peaceful Springs, brought in its report only a couple of hours after the polls closed. It had voted unanimously in favor of keeping the county seat where it was. There were happy smiles among all the Peaceful Springs supporters waiting at the courthouse.

Mapleton had its share of people there, too, awaiting the returns. They didn't seem the least bit disturbed at the unanimous vote from Western Township.

"They know we're going to beat them in the western half of the county," Mary said. "But they think they are so big up in Mapleton that they can win with just their own votes."

"They seemed mighty set on getting those votes from Elkhorn, too," Troy said.

McDuff Township to the northwest, with even fewer votes than Western, reported in with another unanimous No vote. The townships with the larger votes were not in, so no one was celebrating yet.

Troy saw Libby come in with Rudy Yoeman and mingle with the people from Mapleton who were watching the posted returns. Betsy wasn't even there. Maybe she was waiting for Troy to bring her.

A couple of the bigger townships, Winifred and Tower, came in. Winifred, just to the north of Peaceful Springs, went ten to one in favor of keeping things as they were. Tower, between Winifred and Mapleton, gave the edge in their vote to Mapleton. But still the vote was heavily in favor of Peaceful Springs.

When the man rode in with the Elkhorn Township vote, Troy was disappointed. Two to one in favor of Mapleton. There were very few votes for such a big township, and Troy realized that if Peaceful Springs had gotten all the votes he and Willie and Morrie had been taking to the polls today, the margin would not have been so lopsided.

"It's the total that counts," Doris reminded Troy. "We're still far ahead. If we get just a few votes over in Mapleton, we can win."

The votes from the southern townships came in, and they followed the general pattern. The farther west they were, the more in favor of Peaceful Springs; the farther east, the more votes for Mapleton.

It was late when the two voting centers in Mapleton Township made their report. There were so many votes that it had taken much longer to take the count.

Troy crowded close to the desk as the envelopes were opened and the numbers put up on the board. There were some No votes, but the Yes votes ran into the hundreds in both voting wards.

"We're going to have to do some arithmetic to see how this comes out," Doris said as she added up the figures.

Troy was already running the figures through his head. He could see it was going to be mightly close. A few ballots had been blank, and about a hundred and fifty eligible voters had not shown up at the polls. All those counted No. The only figures that really counted were the total number of eligible voters in the county and the number of Yes votes cast.

"How does it come out?" Troy asked, leaning over Doris' shoulder as she did her dividing.

Doris looked up, her face beaming. "They are four votes short. They had to have fourteen hundred and forty-five. They got only fourteen hundred and forty-one."

Troy took a deep breath. "That is too close for comfort."

"But we won," Doris exclaimed. "That means the courthouse stays here. Your hotel will still be in business. And your real estate office will boom now."

"This calls for a celebration," Troy said.

"Let's wait till the sun comes up," Doris said practically, "It's after three o'clock now."

Troy hadn't realized he had spent nearly the entire night at the courthouse. He looked over the room. There were still half as many there as there had been early in the evening. A cheer ran through most of the crowd when it was announced that the Mapleton vote had fallen four short of victory. But there was no cheering from the little knot of Mapleton people. The Mapelton messenger who had brought over the results was still at the desk.

"Well," he said resignedly, "we'll just have to try again in five years. We'll make it next time."

Troy went home with Morrie. He didn't come back to town until noon the next day and found the town celebrating its narrow victory. The streets were as crowded as Troy had seen them for a long time. People who had appeared almost ashamed to be seen in Peaceful Springs were whooping it up. Now that they had won, they were eager to associate themselves with the victors. Troy shook his head as he watched.

He opened his real estate office again and had some potential customers right away. Enthusiasm for buying homes or business sites in Peaceful Springs had suddenly erupted with the news that the county seat was going to stay right where it was.

But Troy found it hard to keep his mind on his business. He would soon be in court to face a murder charge. Amos Brush was working hard to build up a defense, but he frankly admitted that all he really had were character witnesses for Troy. That wasn't enough.

Then, just four days after the election, the county commissioners met and reviewed the election results. Troy was dumbfounded when he heard that the commissioners had gone over the voter list and decided that eleven names on that list were not eligible voters. Some, they said, were incompetent, and others failed to meet residency requirements.

As soon as he heard the news, Troy hurried over to see Mary Willouby. He found her furious, her eyes flashing with anger.

"If this is allowed to stand," Mary stormed, "Mapleton will win the election by two votes. The county commissioners do not have the right to decide who is eligible and who is not. Anyway, that list was made before the election and approved then. They can't change it."

"But they did," Troy said.

"We'll see what a court has to say about that," Mary said angrily.

"What can we do now?" Doris asked. "Mapleton is going to come over here right away and move the records."

"We'll get an injunction against that," Mary said practically. "Then we'll appeal to the courts."

"And also file a suit against the commissioners?" Doris asked. "They overstepped their bounds, didn't they?"

Mary nodded. "We'll file that suit, too."

Troy felt like a bystander, watching the wheels turning. But Mary should know the law, and if she said they had grounds for a suit, he'd go along with her decision.

Troy went back to his office for some papers before heading for the ranch. Willie had been his shadow most of the day, never being right at his side but usually within sight of him. That seemed pointless to Troy. The Detts surely wouldn't try to kill him now. It would mean serious trouble for them. And with the trial only a few days away, they'd be foolish to risk trouble for themselves when the law would do their work for them.

Troy and Willie took their time riding home. It was a nice late fall day, and Troy tried to enjoy it, thinking that he might soon be deprived of freedom like this.

Morrie met them at the corral when they rode into the ranch yard. He had a piece of paper in his hand.

"Another note?" Troy asked.

"This may be just what you're looking for," Morrie said excitedly. "I don't have any idea who left it. But it must be somebody who knows something about Rafe Dett's murder and doesn't want to get involved himself."

Troy grabbed it from Morrie's hand and read it quickly.

"Look in the creek a hundred yards upstream from the place where Rafe was killed. You'll find the gun that killed him."

Troy looked at Willie. "Go back to town and bring out the sheriff. He should still be in his office. I want him there when we find this gun—if it is there."

Willie rode back to town at a fast gallop. Morrie saddled up, and he and Troy were waiting when the sheriff and Willie returned. Troy handed the note to the sheriff.

"Could be a put-up job," the sheriff said skeptically. "But let's go look."

They spent half an hour searching the river above the murder site before Willie, feeling along the bottom of the creek, came up with the gun. The sheriff took it and looked at it carefully.

"You ever have a gun like this?" he asked Troy.

Troy shook his head. "This gun I'm wearing and a .32 Pa gave me when I was a boy are the only ones I've ever had."

The sheriff rubbed his nose. "A .38 on a .45 stock. He was killed with a .38, all right. Your pa had a .38, Troy. Where is it?"

"At the ranch," Troy said. "Come on. I'll show it to you."

They rode back to the ranch, the sheriff keeping the gun they had found in the river.

Inside the house, Troy went to his father's desk and pulled out the drawer where he kept his .38. The gun was there, and Troy handed it to the sheriff. Sheriff Hanson studied it for a moment, then gave it back.

"Could be that this gun was planted in the river by somebody looking for a way to free you from that charge," he said finally. "But it sure has been in the water for a while. Wish I knew who wrote that note."

Troy was wishing the same thing.

"I still think it could be a plant," the sheriff insisted. "But I'll talk to Brush about it."

Two days later Amos Brush rode out to the ranch.

"Got good news for you, Troy," he said. "I showed the gun to the judge and told him we'd have to have more time to try to find out who threw it in the river. This could be the evidence we need to clear you. He agreed to a postponement of your trial until next spring's session. But I've got some bad news, too."

"What's that?" Troy demanded.

"Jake and Ike Dett were raving mad when they found out the trial had been postponed. They are not the kind to wait for what they want. So watch your step."

15.

Betsy came out into the lobby of the hotel while Troy was there. Morrie and Willie were on the hotel porch, watching the town. Betsy's face looked haggard, as if she were just recovering from a sick spell. Troy was shocked.

"I've got to tell you something, Troy," she said. "And I want you to believe it. Rafe Dett did not kill your pa. I was with Rafe over at Tower at a celebration that day. I told you before that I saw Rafe there. It was more than that. I was with him."

"Shut up!" Al Theim shouted. "Don't you dare admit you were with scum like Rafe Dett!"

"I was with him, Pa," Betsy said with spunk. "I'll admit that to anybody. But I won't tell anybody anything else."

She wheeled and went back up the stairs.

Troy left the hotel, going down to see Amos Brush. Brush was optimistic about Troy's chances at his trial in the spring.

"The postponement is our biggest break," he said. "I doubt if the gun will be evidence enough to clear you. But before the spring session of court, something else is bound to happen. Time has a way of uncovering the truth. And time is on our side now."

On the way down the street out of town, Troy was hailed by Vivian Hurley from the door of her dress shop. Troy pulled into the hitchrack, and Willie and Morrie reined in, too.

"I wanted to talk to you, Troy," Vivian said when Troy got inside the shop. "Maybe Betsy isn't your girl any more. I haven't seen you with her lately. But I thought you ought to know that she's been sneaking out of the shop here almost every day and going off on long rides."

"You mean she's not doing her work? Are you going to fire her?"

"I've thought of it," Vivian admitted. "But I've been curious to see who she was riding off to meet. She's not one to ride alone, you know. So I closed the shop yesterday when she left and followed her. She met Rudy Yoeman, and they rode along the river together."

"Yoeman," Troy said, frowning. "That's not much

better than Rafe Dett. Guess she never really was my girl, no matter what I thought. Al will blow sky high if he finds out about this. Is Betsy here now?"

"No. She just reported for work, then went right out. She has told me that she doesn't want any pay for the time she isn't here. She's just using this job to keep her folks from finding out what she's doing. I don't know whether I should tell them or not."

"Hold off till I talk to her," Troy said. "Have you told Libby? She's supposed to have Rudy tied up. Seems to me she's being double-crossed worse than Al and Emma Theim."

Vivian nodded. "Maybe. But I'm not about to tell Libby. We've been good friends for a long time. I'm not going to risk that friendship by telling her something she might not believe. Anyway, I doubt if Betsy means anything to Rudy."

Troy went back outside.

"I'm going to stick around town for a while," he told Morrie and Willie. "Betsy is out riding. I want to talk to her when she gets back."

Betsy didn't return to the dress shop until just before closing time. Then she walked to the hotel as if she were just leaving work. Troy met her half a block from the hotel.

"I hear you've been riding around with Rudy Yoeman," he said, not trying to keep the anger out of his voice.

"What if I am?" Betsy flared. "I'm old enough to pick my own companions. I haven't seen you around lately to keep me busy."

"Maybe Rudy has good reason to kidnap you."

Betsy's face turned livid. "Oh, I hate you!" she screamed, and slapped him across the face, then ran toward the hotel.

He'd bungled the meeting, but he didn't really care. He had found out that Vivian had been telling the truth. Troy had started toward his horse when Al Theim came running out of the hotel and overtook him.

"What did you say to Betsy?" he demanded. "She's madder than a hen in a horse tank."

"I heard she'd been riding around with Rudy Yoeman," Troy said. "I just wanted to find out if it was true."

"It ain't!" Theim shouted. "It can't be."

"Ask her," Troy said, and swung into the saddle.

Al Theim practically jumped up and down in his rage. "I'll kill him!" he sputtered.

He was still sputtering and swearing when Troy rode out of town with his two bodyguards. Now that Rafe Dett had an alibi, he pondered the question: who had killed Frank! Suddenly Troy had the answer. Rudy Yoeman. He should have thought of that before.

Yoeman had been staying at the ranch with Rafe at

the time. And there was nobody else near Peaceful Springs who would want Frank Prescott dead. With Frank dead, Rudy probably figured it would be easy to get his ranch, and that would give the Detts control of all the land southeast of town. Since Rudy expected to marry Libby and inherit a big chunk of the Dett land, that certainly gave him a motive for killing Frank.

After supper, Troy went to his room early, which was not unusual for him. But as soon as Willie had gone to the bunkhouse and Morrie had settled down in the front part of the house, Troy went through the window and circled around to the corral.

Quietly he saddled his horse and led him out on the grass beyond the corral. He didn't mount until he was well out of earshot of the ranch. It took only a short time to get to the Dett ranch. He left the horse at the far side of the corral and moved quietly up to the house. Peering in the window, he saw Norge and Hilda Uldeen sitting near the table where the lamp was lit. He saw nothing of either Yoeman or Libby. That was the way he wanted it.

Stepping up to the door, he knocked. A moment later, Hilda Uldeen opened the door. She stared at Troy, frowning.

"What do you want?"

"Just to talk a minute," Troy said softly. "Anybody else here?"

"Just Norge. Libby has gone to bed, like we're getting ready to do."

"Where's Rudy Yoeman?" Troy asked.

"I don't keep no tabs on him. He ain't here now, if it's him you're looking for."

"I want to talk to you and Norge," Troy said, and stepped inside. He moved directly to the table where Norge sat, staring at him. It appeared to Troy that Norge was sober for once.

"I want to find out what you know about Rudy Yoeman," Troy said.

"I don't have to answer any questions," Norge grunted. "He draws his pay here just like the rest of us. Ask him what you want to know."

"What did he do before he came here to work?" Troy asked, ignoring Uldeen's reluctance to talk.

Uldeen grimaced. "He was a bookkeeper in a store in Mapleton. He and Rafe were good drinking buddies. So when Rafe came over here to run this place, Rudy came along. Wanted to make a good impression on Libby and her pa, I reckon."

Troy nodded. "Did Rudy stay on the ranch when Rafe was gone?" he asked.

Uldeen shrugged. "I don't know nothing about what he did till we got here. I know he ain't worth a bull's bellow in a blizzard when it comes to work. I figure he's planning on taking over this end of Jake's holdings. Libby is to inherit this land at Peaceful Springs, now that Rafe is dead. And Rudy is set on marrying Libby."

"He may get suckered out of what he thinks he's going to get like we were," Hilda said angrily.

Hilda's anger was contagious. "Jake's good at that, all right," Norge said hotly. "Got us working for him when we ought to own half of what he's got."

Troy frowned. "Were you partners with Jake?"

"Jake didn't have a cow to milk or a bucket to put it in till Harriet's and Hilda's pa died and left them what he had. He got Harriet's half, of course, then stole Hilda's half."

"He knew Norge loved cards but couldn't handle his whiskey," Hilda added as if she had to give vent to her fury. "So he got him drunk, then played poker with him. Got everything I had inherited. Made it stick legally, too." Her fists clenched. "Some day I'm going to get it back somehow!"

"Then you don't know whether Rudy stayed here at the ranch on the days that Rafe was gone?"

Hilda shrugged. "I don't know what he did, but I reckon Jake gave orders for somebody to stay here all the time. That's our orders now, anyway. So he probably was here when Rafe was gone. What difference does it make?"

"None, maybe," Troy said. "Thanks for talking to me."

"Jake would rather have us kill you," Hilda said.

Troy went to the door and let himself out. Getting his horse, he rode away from the buildings, heading toward his own ranch.

He felt the blow in his upper left chest before he heard the shot. It jerked him out of the saddle and slammed him to the ground.

He didn't lose consciousness and, gasping for breath, he rolled to the side of the road into the weeds. He heard a horse come up out of a ravine beside the road. Whoever had shot him apparently was coming to make sure of his job.

16.

Troy lay as still as possible, trying to keep his ragged breathing silent. The rider came up on the road and stopped beside Troy's horse, which had gone on about twenty yards after Troy fell off. Then he moved slowly up the road in Troy's direction.

But suddenly he stopped. A moment later, he wheeled his horse and spurred him in the opposite direction. Troy didn't understand, and things were getting so fuzzy he didn't really care.

Then he heard someone running up the road from the direction of the buildings. Vaguely Troy realized that someone at the house must have heard the shot and be coming to investigate.

Fighting the blackness that was crowding in on him, Troy tried to move back to the road. But he couldn't manage it. He must have rustled the grass in his effort, though, because whoever was running down the road turned directly toward the spot where he was lying.

He expected to see either Norge or Hilda Uldeen. But it was Libby. She knelt and examined the wound in his upper chest, then wheeled toward someone who had been following her.

"Uncle Norge," she called, "get the wagon and a team."

Troy tried to hold onto consciousness, but it was no use. Blackness moved in, blotting out Libby's face as she leaned over him. . . .

The jolt of the wagon brought him back to reality. He groaned at the pain. Libby shifted a pillow under his head.

"Who shot you?" she asked.

Troy's wits were coming back rapidly. "Yoeman, I think," he said.

"Impossible," Libby said, anger driving out the softness of a moment before. "Rudy wouldn't do anything like this. Anyway, he went over to see Ike. He didn't plan to come back till tomorrow."

Troy knew better than to insist.

"Where are we going?" he asked, surprised at how weak his voice was.

"We're taking you home," Libby said. "Aunt Hilda is driving the wagon, and we sent Uncle Norge for a doctor."

LAW OF THE PRAIRIE

When the wagon rattled into the yard at the ranch, Morrie and Willie met it, both dressed only in pants and boots. After expressing their opinions about Troy slipping out on them, Willie put Troy's horse away, while Morrie helped get Troy into the house and to bed.

Libby stayed with Troy until Norge arrived with a doctor from Winifred, about twelve miles northwest of Peaceful Springs. The doctor gave Troy something that knocked him out while he probed for the bullet.

When Troy came to, the doctor was gone, but Libby was still sitting by the bed. She leaned over Troy when she saw that he was awake.

"Doc says you were lucky. The bullet didn't hit anything vital. You'll pull through, but you'll have to be quiet for quite a while."

Troy looked at Libby for a long time. When he spoke, his words were barely a whisper. "Why did you stay here?"

"I wanted to make sure you did wake up," she said. "For a while, we weren't sure you would. Anyway, you got shot practically in my yard, so I feel some responsibility. Now that you're able to ask such silly questions, I guess you can get along by yourself. I'll be up to see you once in a while."

"I'll like that," Troy said.

Morrie and Willie took turns sitting with Troy

during the day, giving him a little laudanum once when the pain got bad. When night came, Morrie bedded down on a cot pulled into Troy's room.

Troy was able to sit up in bed by the evening when Mary and Doris rode out to tell him that the judge had reversed his position and declared that the county commissioners had not had the right to remove any names from the official list of eligible voters in the county. So Peaceful Springs had won the election.

"Makes me feel like getting right out of bed and dancing a jig," Troy said. "Maybe things will pick up in town now."

"Maybe," Mary said dubiously. "Mapleton isn't going to take this decision lying down. It's gone so far now that, whichever way the lower courts decide, the losers are going to appeal to the state supreme court. That's where the final decision is going to be made."

"You're not planning on a big celebration?" Troy asked.

"I think the town will throw a shindig, all right, but I'm going to save my celebrating until we know for sure we're going to hold the county seat."

"Hope I can be there for the celebration," Troy said. "Right now I've got to get on my feet and run down the man who ambushed me."

"You'd better find the man who killed Rafe Dett," Doris said. "Your trial will be coming up soon."

Troy got out of bed the next day without waiting for the doctor's permission. But he was too weak and dizzy to walk, and Morrie had to help him back to bed.

Each day after that he got up and was soon moving around. He was in the kitchen when Mary drove into the yard in her buggy. When she came into the house, he could see that she was bearing bad news.

"The judge reversed himself again," she announced without preliminaries. "He struck those eleven names off the eligible voter list. So as of now, Mapleton is the winner. We're going to appeal to the state supreme court, of course."

"Think it will do any good?" Troy asked.

"I don't know. We've got to try. We won't have much left in Peaceful Springs if we lose the courthouse."

"I won't have any business at all," Troy said. "Guess I haven't had any real estate business, anyway. Can't sell much land from a bed."

Two days later, Troy got on a horse for the first time since he'd been shot. He didn't ride far. The jolting hurt his chest and shoulder too much. But he knew he could stay in the saddle now if it was necessary. In a few days, he could go where he wanted to.

Mary and Doris came out a few evenings later. Troy had ridden three miles that day and had decided that tomorrow he was going to start looking for evidence against Rudy Yoeman. But the news Mary and Doris brought pushed Yoeman to the back of his mind.

"The Kansas supreme court ruled in favor of Mapleton," Mary announced hopelessly. "Looks like we've lost the county seat."

"Nothing any higher we can go to, I reckon," Troy said.

"The U.S. supreme court would hardly consider a little county seat fight. So I guess this is it."

"When will they move the records?"

"Knowing the ones pushing this move, I'd guess they won't lose any time. Could you spare Morrie tomorrow to come into town and help us keep an eye on things? Wouldn't surprise me if they tried to carry off the whole town while they were at it."

"Sure," Troy said. "Might come in myself, too. I've got plenty of interest in that town."

Morrie rode off at sunrise the next morning to stay in town for the day. Willie tried to convince Troy to keep out of town.

"I figure Jake and Ike Dett will be with whoever comes for those records," Willie said. "Moving the county seat is only part of what they want. They want you dead, too."

"I'll wait a while before I go in," Troy conceded "Might get pretty tired if I tried to stick it out all day, anyway."

Willie went out to the bunkhouse just as Libby rode in. She hadn't even heard of the supreme court decision and she didn't seem overjoyed when Troy told her.

"Pa said nothing could be touched until all the court decisions were out of the way," she said. "That supreme court decision wipes out all the others, doesn't it?"

"That's the way Mary figures. They're expecting the people from Mapleton over today to get the records."

Troy didn't hear any sound until Rudy Yoeman suddenly appeared in the doorway. He had a gun in his hand.

Troy stared at Yoeman; then his eyes flashed to the window. He saw Willie lying stretched out at the corner of the bunkhouse.

"Did you kill Willie?" Troy shouted angrily.

"Only put him to sleep for a while," Yoeman said. "He's not the one I'm after."

"What are you doing, Rudy!" Libby demanded.

Yoeman scowled at Libby. "How long have you been sneaking out and coming over here to snuggle up to this killer? I saw you leave this morning and followed you."

"It's none of your business," Libby snapped. "Now you get out of here."

"Hold on, Libby," Yoeman said soothingly. "Are

166

you standing up for him against me? We're the ones getting married, I thought."

"Not if you do what you're thinking of doing," Libby shot back. "I won't marry a killer."

"Now you listen to me," Yoeman said. "He's accusing me of killing his old man. I'm not going to stand for that."

Libby looked at Troy. "Have you accused him of that?"

"I've been considering it," Troy said. "Looks like I'm right. He wouldn't want to kill me now if he wasn't guilty."

Yoeman turned his gun on Troy and tried to move around Libby. But she stayed between Yoeman and Troy.

"Rudy, don't be an idiot!" she shouted. "If you kill him, I'll be a witness."

"But you won't tell anybody."

"I will," she said. Then, faster than the wind, she had a little gun out of her pocket. "I don't want to use this gun on you, Rudy. But so help me, I will if you don't get out of here."

Yoeman stared at Libby in astonishment, his mouth dropping open. "I believe you actually would. You little spitfire!"

"Get out, Rudy. We'll talk about this when you cool down."

Yoeman stood his ground for a moment, hesitation in his face.

"Now, Libby," he said coaxingly, "you know I wouldn't do anything that you didn't want me to." He holstered his gun and backed to the door. "Come on home with me, Libby."

"I'll be along," Libby said. "You go ahead."

She stayed close to Troy as Yoeman backed outside. Through the window, Troy saw him go to his horse, mount and ride off toward town.

"Got to see how bad Willie is hurt," Troy said, and ran to the door.

Willie was just starting to stir when Troy reached him. He sat up, holding his head.

"What hit me?" he asked.

"Rudy Yoeman. Must have sneaked up behind the bunkhouse and clouted you as you came around the corner."

Willie stared at Troy. "How come you're alive? He must have been after you."

"Libby talked him out of it," Troy said. "You going to be all right?"

"Sure," Willie said, getting to his feet but hanging onto the corner of the bunkhouse like a seasick sailor.

"I've got some things to do," Troy said, and ran back to the house.

He still felt a little weak, but he couldn't yield to

that weakness now. Inside the house, he got his gun belt and made sure his gun was loaded and the belt loops full of ammunition. As he started out the door again, Libby stopped him.

"Where are you going?"

"After Yoeman," Troy said. "I'm positive he killed my pa. And I'm sure he bushwhacked me, too. I'm going to get some answers from him."

"You're no better than he is!" Libby said hotly.

"Maybe not," Troy said. "But I've got to have some answers, and I figure he's the one to give them to me. I'm sorry if you don't agree."

He pushed past Libby and hurried to the corral. Willie was still leaning against the bunkhouse. He wasn't going to be in any condition to stop Troy. Saddling his horse, Troy rode out of the yard toward town. As he left, he saw Libby going toward her horse.

At the bridge crossing Spring Creek at the edge of town, Troy met Al Theim, spurring his horse down from the hotel. Troy held up a hand, and Theim slid his horse to a halt.

"What's wrong with you?" Troy demanded.

"Betsy just rode off with that Yoeman fellow. He's up to no good. I'm going after them."

Before Troy could stop him, he spurred his horse past Troy and on to the south. Troy was about to wheel after him, knowing he'd find Yoeman in that direction, when he saw Emma Theim running down the street toward him. He nudged his horse toward her.

"Al's crazy," Emma panted. "Can you stop him?"

"I doubt it," Troy said. "He seems set on bringing Betsy back."

"That's what he went out to do the day he killed Rafe Dett," Emma said.

"Al killed Rafe?" Troy said with a gasp.

"Betsy was running around with Rafe, and Al is wildly jealous of anybody who looks at Betsy. That is, everybody except you." Her eyes fell from Troy's face. "Al should have said something when you were arrested. I should have, too. But Al and Betsy are all I've got, and the law couldn't have convicted you, anyway. Now Al will kill Rudy Yoeman—or get killed. Can't you do something, Troy?"

Troy's mind was still grappling with the news Emma had brought. It suddenly struck him that his only chance of clearing himself of Rafe Dett's murder was to keep Al Theim alive. He wheeled his horse and dug in the spurs.

17.

Troy was almost to the Smoky Hill River when he saw a horse grazing on a hill ahead. As he got closer, he saw that the horse was saddled. And before he reached it, he recognized it as the one Al Theim had been riding when he had left town just a short time ago.

Reining up near the horse, his eyes scanned the surrounding prairie. Then he saw Al Theim down in the ravine not far away. Troy nudged his horse that way.

Swinging out of the saddle, he knelt beside the hotel operator. He had been shot in the chest at close range. Al Theim was dead. And with his death, Troy's one sure way of clearing himself of Rafe Dett's murder was gone. Now all he had was Emma Theim's testimony. And she might refuse to talk just to protect the

171

memory of her weak-spined husband.

Troy swung into the saddle and rode on, leaning over occasionally to make sure he was following the tracks of the two horses ahead of him. Surely Betsy wasn't going willingly with Yoeman now that he had murdered her father.

Then, after crossing the river, he found Betsy standing by her horse, crying. Troy reined up beside her.

"Where did Yoeman go?" he demanded.

"What do you care?" Betsy said between sobs. "He shot Pa. Then he refused to take me with him any farther. Said I'd just be in his way."

"You mean you wanted to go with him?"

"He promised me we'd always be together," Betsy sobbed. "That was before Pa came charging out here like a madman and told Rudy he was going to kill him. Rudy had no choice. He had to kill Pa."

"I figure he also killed my pa," Troy said. "And he almost got me too."

Betsy nodded, brushing tears from her face. "He admitted that he killed your pa, but it was just because he wouldn't sell his land so the Detts could connect their ranches. Rudy said some day we'd own all this land south of town."

"Just how did you figure he was going to do that?" Troy asked disgustedly. "The only way he can get this

Dett land is to marry Libby. That wouldn't leave much place for you, would it?"

Troy could see that Betsy hadn't thought of that before.

"You'd better get back to town and comfort your ma," he said. "She's going to take this pretty hard."

Troy kicked his horse into a trot. He had expected Yoeman to go to the ranch south of town. But the tracks of the horse suddenly swung northeast.

The sun swung over the zenith and had started down the western sky when Troy came in sight of Jake Dett's buildings, almost a mile away on the flat prairie. He reined up and studied the terrain. Yoeman's tracks led straight to the buildings. But Troy couldn't ride in directly. He'd never make it. If Rudy Yoeman didn't kill him, Ike or Jake Dett surely would.

There was a ravine off to his left that ran behind the buildings. Nudging his horse over into the ravine, Troy kept his head low as he rode toward the Dett buildings. He was perhaps halfway there, and the ravine was deep enough so that he was beginning to feel fairly secure, when he was brought up short by a sharp voice above him.

"Hold up!"

Troy jerked his head up to stare into the bore of Ike Dett's gun. Ike was riding a big bay horse, and there was no surprise on his face. He obviously had seen Troy as soon as he had appeared to the southwest of the buildings and had ridden out to intercept him.

"Come on up here," Ike ordered, and Troy reined his horse up the steep incline to the level of the prairie.

"What are you doing here?" Ike demanded, jerking Troy's gun out of its holster.

"Looking for Rudy Yoeman," Troy said. "He killed my father and bushwhacked me. I figure I owe him something. He also killed Al Theim earlier this morning. It was Theim who killed Rafe, not me."

Ike's expression showed little surprise. "I suppose you think we'll believe you didn't kill Rafe? It's easy to blame a man who is dead and can't defend himself." Ike jerked the muzzle of his gun toward the barn. "Come on and talk to Pa."

Troy nudged his horse into motion.

"Is Rudy Yoeman here?" he asked as they reached the corrals and dismounted.

"What if he is?" Ike asked sullenly.

"Norge Uldeen tells me Yoeman is planning to take over all the Dett land around Peaceful Springs for his own."

Ike scowled. At last Troy had said something that Ike hadn't heard before. "Just how does he figure on doing that?"

"By marrying Libby," Troy said. "He may have

174

some other scheme to go with that."

"What's Libby's belongs to Libby, not Rudy," Ike said. "I reckon it will stay that way."

Troy knew better than to press the subject. If Ike told Yoeman what he'd said already, it would only add fuel to Yoeman's determination to kill Troy.

Halfway to the house, Jake came out and met them. He glared at Troy, then at Ike. "Why didn't you kill him out there?" Jake demanded.

"He still ain't signed over that land to us," Ike said. "He says it was Theim who killed Rafe. Even if that's so, we've still got to get that land."

Jake nodded his head slowly. "We'd be fools to pass up a chance like this. Put him down in the cellar. We'll figure out a way to get him to sign."

"Let Rudy persuade him," Ike said with a grin. "He's got more reason to kill him now than we have."

"We've got plenty," Jake said.

Ike prodded Troy toward the cellar behind the house. The door was on a slope so water would run off it. Once opened, it revealed steep steps down into the musty, dark interior. Ike struck a match and lit a candle. It gave enough light so that he could see to tie Troy with some ropes he had brought along. There was an old cottonwood stump on the dirt floor, and Troy was seated on that, close enough to the damp wall so that he could lean back against it.

"Reckon that will hold you till we decide what to do," Ike said. He blew out the candle, then went back up the steps and closed the door.

It seemed to be pitch-dark inside the cellar. But after a couple of minutes, Troy's eyes grew accustomed to the darkness, and he noticed a thread of light filtering down from a hole in the roof. This ventilation hole apparently had a shield over the top so neither rain nor direct sunlight could get in, but it did allow a little light inside, noticeable only when a man's eyes were accustomed to the darkness.

Some time later the outside door opened, and Ike came down the steps. He had a bowl of soup and meat, and he lit the candle, then untied Troy's hands so he could eat. Ike leaned against the wall with his gun in his hand. Troy considered making a break while his hands were free. But his feet were still tied, and he was sure Ike was just waiting for him to make a move.

"We'll let you stew here tonight," Ike said when Troy had finished his supper. "Pa says we're not going to wait for the bank to foreclose on that land of yours. We're going to get you to sign it over; then we'll pay off the mortgage. It will still make cheap land for us. After you've spent a night down here with the rats, maybe you'll decide you'd rather be topside, even if you don't own any land."

Troy didn't bother to answer. After Ike had tied his

hands again and blown out the candle, he went up the steps and shut the door. Deep darkness closed in on Troy.

He checked the ropes on his wrists. Ike had done a good job. Troy had looked around him while the candle had been lit. There were some jars on shelves only a few feet to his right. If he could get over there and break one of those jars, he might use some broken pieces of glass to cut the ropes.

He dozed part of the night, but his mind kept working on ideas on how to escape.

A faint light filtering through the vent announced daylight. Troy strained his eyes to see the jars on the shelves. But he still hadn't managed to distinguish anything but the tiny hole in the ceiling when the outside door suddenly opened with a squeak.

Ike came down the steps again with a bowl of food. Once more he lit the candle and untied Troy's hands. Troy shot a glance at Ike. Ike was watching him eagerly.

Troy gave him no excuse to use his gun. He ate very slowly, looking around the cellar, trying to memorize every detail of his surroundings.

Then suddenly someone came running across the yard and stopped at the top of the cellar steps.

"Ike, you down there?"

"Sure, Pa," Ike said. "What's wrong?"

"I've been robbed. Has that varmint down there been loose?"

"Course not," Ike yelled back. "He wouldn't be here if he'd got loose. Who robbed you and what did he get?"

"He got the money out of my box under the bed. Four thousand dollars. Have you seen Rudy this morning?"

Ike swore lustily. "No. That dirty skunk must have robbed you, then skipped out."

Ike jerked the bowl of food from Troy's hands, then yanked his hands behind him, quickly tying the rope in place. Then he blew out the candle and ran up the steps, three at a time.

The outside door slammed shut, and Troy knew he'd be there for a long while without food or water. The Detts had something more urgent to take care of than feeding a prisoner.

18.

Troy heard muffled sounds in the yard as men ran about. Then, as he leaned against the wall of the cellar, he felt the vibration of horses' hoofs.

Troy knew that now was his best chance of getting away, if he had any chance at all. It would be a while before Ike and Jake came back.

He tested the ropes on his wrists. They were not as tight as before. Ike had been in too big a hurry when he'd tied him this time. For five minutes, Troy tried to work his hands out of the ropes, but he couldn't quite do it.

He stood up on his bound feet, thinking that he'd try to break a jar and use the glass to cut the ropes. But he promptly fell; his legs were too numb to hold him up. He hit a couple of large stone jars he had seen not far from the stump he'd been sitting on. He hadn't considered what might be in those jars. Each had a tin lid on it, held down by a rock. When he fell, he upset one of the jars and knocked the lid away.

The strong odor of lard struck his nostrils and he realized the jars were full of lard from the last hog butchering, and the tin lids had been held on top to keep mice out of the lard.

An idea hit Troy. Jabbing his hands into the jar, he worked them into the lard. Then he rubbed his hands together, moving the grease up over his wrists and the ropes. Within two minutes, he had slipped his greased hands out of the ropes. Using a sack he had felt under him when he fell, he wiped off all the lard he could. Then he set about untying the ropes around his ankles with numbed fingers.

It took him five minutes of rubbing to restore the circulation in his ankles and feet. His hands were better, because they hadn't been immobile so long.

Then he moved to the outside door and pushed against it. It was as heavy as he had expected it to be.

Once he budged it, however, the counterweight helped him lift it a foot in the air. He stopped pushing, wondering if the squeak that the counterweight made would be heard in the house. Harriet Dett, Jake's wife, was surely there.

Nothing stirred in the yard, and Troy lifted the door higher and slipped outside, letting the door down as quietly as possible. He moved over against the house and stood there, waiting to see if anybody came out of the house.

No one did, and Troy looked toward the corral. He saw his horse, and there were saddles on the fence. Somehow he had to get to his horse and get him saddled without being detected.

Dodging from one building to another, he got to the corral from the other side and climbed over the fence. There were half a dozen horses inside, but he called to his horse, and the horse waited for him to move up and grab his mane. Leading him to the corral fence, he bridled him, then threw his saddle on him.

He had the cinch almost tightened when he heard a shrill yell from the house. He didn't even look up, but finished the cinch and, grabbing the bridle reins, pulled his horse toward the gate.

Jerking open the gate, he swung into the saddle just as a rifle roared. The bullet missed, but he saw the woman just outside the door of the house jack another cartridge into the chamber.

Leaning low over the saddle, he kicked his heels into his horse's flanks and sent him out of the yard at a hard gallop. The rifle bellowed twice more but no bullet hit him, and his horse didn't falter in his stride.

Then he was out of the range of the rifle, riding southwest. He saw that he was going in the same direction in which several horses had traveled not long before. Apparently Rudy Yoeman had gone that way, and Jake and Ike were following.

Troy eased his horse back to a gait he could keep up for many miles. He was free again, but he didn't even have a gun. If he ran into either Rudy Yoeman or the Detts, he'd be a dead man.

He had to get to Peaceful Springs and get a gun.

He found the town almost deserted as he rode down the main street. But to the west, he could see people swarming around the courthouse.

Troy stopped at his real estate office and fished in his pocket. Ike hadn't taken his keys, and now Troy unlocked the door. Getting the .32, he stuffed it in his waistband and hurried back to his horse.

He was approaching the crowd around the courthouse when Doris Jewel saw him and came running his way.

"Where have you been?" she asked, then went on without waiting for an answer. "You should see what they did to the courthouse when they came for the records."

Troy nodded and swung off his horse. "Maybe I should."

He followed Doris, who led him at a trot toward the front door. There were whiskey bottles and boxes and boards all over the lawn.

"Must have been some drunken spree they had," Troy said, his anger rising.

"It was," Doris said. "Looks like they were either too lazy or too drunk to carry out everything. See that broken window in the clerk's office? Must have thrown some of the stuff out that way."

"Why did they have to destroy everything?" Troy asked.

"Wait till you see what they did inside!" Doris said.

At the door, they met Mary, who turned and went inside with Troy and Doris. Troy stopped and stared when they went into Mary's office. There was a vault there built of fireproof bricks, and it had had a heavy steel door. The door was gone now, and a big gaping hole was in its place. Bricks were strewn around as if they had somehow simply ripped the door out.

"Why in the world did they do that?" Troy demanded.

Mary could scarcely control her fury. "They say they're going to use the vault doors in the new courthouse," she said. "But I'll bet they never do. They just wanted to destroy everything here. The yard looks worse than an uncleaned pig pen."

"There's nothing so destructive as people when they want to be," Doris said more calmly. "You should see the other rooms. They're torn up just about like this one."

Troy fought down his fury. "I've seen enough. Is this why everybody is up here instead of downtown?"

Mary nodded. "If anybody from that gang who came over from Mapleton showed up here right now, he'd likely get shot. People are that mad. We knew they were coming for the records, and nobody tried to stop them. But they had no call to do what they did."

"They must have sent over the scum of Mapleton to get the records," Doris said.

Libby Dett came into Mary's office from another room. "I just can't imagine people from Mapleton doing what they did here," she said. "They must have hired a bunch of no-good drunken bums to do their work."

"Don't tell me you're mad about it, too," Troy said.

"I sure am," Libby said quickly. "I plan to live in this community. And this courthouse was a fine building. There was absolutely no sense in destroying it."

Vivian Hurley came to the door. "There's a man out here who wants to see you, Libby," she said hesitantly.

Libby nodded and followed Vivian outside. Troy stood staring at the destruction in the room.

"I wonder who wants to see Libby," Mary said. "Vivian seemed a little reluctant to tell her."

Troy went to the window and looked out. It took him a while to locate Libby. Then he saw her over at the edge of the crowd, talking to Rudy Yoeman. It was obvious they were arguing.

"It's Yoeman," Troy said, turning to the door. "I've been trying to catch him. He was the one who killed Pa, not Rafe Dett. And he killed Al Theim, too."

Troy ran out of the room and worked his way through the crowd in the entryway to the outside door. Staring out over the crowd from the steps of the courthouse, he saw Yoeman practically pulling Libby toward the hitchrack, where the saddled horses were standing crowded together.

Troy shoved his way through the crowd to the hitchrack. But by the time he got there, Yoeman and Libby were mounted and racing south out of town. Troy ran to his horse, jerked the reins loose and leaped into the saddle.

Once free of the congestion of horses, buggies and buckboards, Troy lined out after Yoeman and Libby. Now he could see that Yoeman had the reins of Libby's horse and was pulling him along at a fast gallop, while Libby was trying to jerk the reins free.

Troy dug in his heels. Yoeman was going to have his hands full. Libby was not one to give up easily. Although she couldn't get her horse free from Yoeman, she was dragging him back, holding down his speed. Troy gained quickly on the two. Yoeman saw Troy coming and jerked out his gun, but he didn't shoot. Libby was almost directly in line with Troy.

Yoeman and Libby splashed across the Smoky Hill and headed south. Troy followed, but now he held back. If he got too close, he would make a good target for Yoeman, and he wouldn't dare shoot back for fear of hitting Libby.

A little over a mile south of town, a butte that someone had named Castle Rock rose abruptly out of the prairie. Its yellow rock had withstood the eroding forces of nature for centuries after all the rock around it had melted away into the prairie.

Yoeman reined in behind the rock, and Troy spurred his horse toward the protection of the near side. If Yoeman dismounted and got a steady shot at Troy from the ground, he could hardly miss.

Troy was almost to the rock when he saw Yoeman step out into the open with his gun. But Libby leaped at him, hitting him just as he fired, sending the bullet skyward.

Troy changed directions and bore straight in on Yoeman. Yoeman was struggling to free himself from Libby and finally managed to knock her backwards. But when he turned to bring his gun to bear on Troy, Troy was driving his horse straight at him. Yoeman had to dive to one side to avoid the horse.

Leaping from the saddle, Troy wheeled toward Yoeman, hitting him just as he was bringing up the gun again. Troy didn't even try for the .32 in his waistband. Grabbing Yoeman's arm above the wrist, he twisted it around until the gun was pointed at the big rock. When Yoeman involuntarily squeezed the trigger, yellow dust spurted from a spot near the top of the rock.

Then Troy brought Yoeman's arm down over his leg and snapped the gun free. Yoeman jerked away and backed off to get his balance. Yoeman was the same height as Troy but several pounds heavier. He was desperate, but his desperation was matched by Troy's fury.

They stood toe to toe and slugged viciously for a full minute. Then Yoeman backed off and circled warily, apparently looking for an advantage he hadn't found in the match of strength.

Troy felt weariness sweeping over him. The blows he had taken from Yoeman had had their effect, and his wound was hurting fiercely. He hadn't regained all his strength yet, either. He tried to shake off his weariness. If he lost this fight, he knew he wouldn't live to try again.

Then Yoeman stumbled over a rock that had chipped off the big butte. Stooping, he swept the rock into his hand in one motion and swung his arm around, aiming the rock at Troy's head.

Troy waited until Yoeman started to throw the rock, then lunged at Yoeman's knees. The rock sailed over his head.

Troy hit Yoeman's legs, and they went down, Yoeman on top. For a minute, they rolled over the rocky ground like two dogs in a battle to the death. Finally Yoeman broke away and got to his feet. Troy lunged up, too, but his strength was about gone; his knees were trembling. If this fight lasted much longer, he would drop from exhaustion. Yoeman couldn't help seeing that.

Troy stepped back to catch his breath, and Yoeman apparently thought he saw the advantage he'd been looking for. He charged forward like a blind bull. Troy quickly stepped aside, meeting Yoeman's charge with all the strength he could put behind his fist. He hit him squarely in the middle of his face, splitting his lips and mashing his nose.

Yoeman howled and fell back. Troy summoned all his remaining strength and went after him, hammering Yoeman's face as he fell backward. Then Troy got one clean shot at his chin and put his last ounce of strength into it. If that failed, he was finished.

Yoeman's head snapped backward, and he rocked back on his heels, staggered to catch himself, then sagged forward, falling on his face.

Troy wobbled over to the base of the butte and leaned there, slowly sinking to the ground himself. Libby ran to Troy and dropped on her knees.

"Are you hurt bad?" she asked, dabbing at some

blood at the corner of his mouth.

"I'll survive," Troy mumbled. "How about Rudy?"

Libby turned and sent a glance at Yoeman, but he wasn't stirring. Then she turned back to Troy just as the drum of hoofbeats came from the far side of the rock. Sheriff Robert Hanson came pounding around the butte and jerked back on the reins.

"Looks like you took care of things yourself," he said to Troy after surveying the scene. "Doris saw you ride out and told me. I came as fast as I could."

"You're a couple of minutes late, Sheriff." Troy managed a sickly grin. "But I guess I enjoyed pounding him up a little." His face sobered. "He killed my pa, Sheriff. He also killed Al Theim. And it was Al who killed Rafe Dett."

The sheriff nodded. "Al's dead. But Yoeman has a long stretch in prison ahead of him if he lives that long. Feel like riding back now?"

"Sure," Troy said, and struggled to his feet, Libby helping him.

The sheriff went to Rudy Yoeman, who was just beginning to regain his senses, and took him at the point of his gun to his horse. Troy and Libby mounted their horses and rode slowly back toward town. Sheriff Hanson went ahead with Yoeman.

Troy and Libby dropped farther behind the sheriff and his prisoner. At the river, they stopped their horses.

"I haven't thanked you for coming to get me away from Rudy," Libby said.

"Hold on," Troy objected. "I'm still in debt to you. You saved my neck there at the dugout and again when I was shot close to your place. And just where do you think I'd be now if you hadn't hit Rudy when he was trying to shoot me just a few minutes ago?"

"Let's just call it even."

"If we're going to keep on looking out for each other, maybe we ought to make it a permanent arrangement," Troy said.

Libby's black eyes studied him for a moment. "Do you mean anything special by that?"

"Something very special," he said.

She smiled and leaned from the saddle to meet his kiss. When he nudged his horse into the stream, his world wore a golden halo and his bruises were forgotten.

The crowd was still on the courthouse lawn when Troy and Libby rode up. But most of the people were pressed around the jail where Sheriff Hanson had just taken Rudy Yoeman. Troy saw Jake and Ike Dett riding up the street from the main part of town. Libby nudged her horse over to cut off her father and brother.

"The sheriff has Rudy now," she said. "Let the law take care of him."

Jake scowled at her, then looked past her at Troy. "When did you take to riding around with him?" he demanded.

"We've been together more than we planned to be," Libby said. "But from now on, we're going to be together because we plan to be. We're getting married, Pa."

Jake's jaw dropped. "Married? You and this—this—"

"This son-in-law of yours," Libby said, smiling. "You know now he didn't kill Rafe. You owe him something for an apology. How about a wedding present?"

Troy thought Jake was going to have apoplexy. He sputtered unintelligibly.

"When we add my place to Troy's, we'll have a very nice ranch," Libby added.

"Your place?" Jake exploded.

· "You said this ranch at Peaceful Springs would be mine some day," Libby said. "You can make it our wedding present."

Ike had just sat his saddle as if paralyzed by the news. Now he grunted. "I sure hate to have him for a brother-in-law. But I reckon that won't be any worse than a thief like Rudy."

It was more of an apology than Troy had ever expected to get from Ike Dett. Jake was still staring at

191

LAW OF THE PRAIRIE

his daughter as if he'd lost his last friend. Finally he let his breath out like an explosion.

"All right," he said. "I reckon you can have the ranch. But it sure is going to be tough having grandchildren named Prescott.

He reined around and rode back down the street with Ike. Troy turned to Libby.

"Grandchildren?"

"First things first," Libby said quickly. "How about a marriage license?"

Troy grinned. Then he looked at the old courthouse. "We'll have to go to Mapleton to get that now."

"Oh, well, with the county seat moved, there won't be so many people here," Libby said. "We don't want too many people crowded around our ranch, anyway, do we?"

"We don't," Troy agreed.